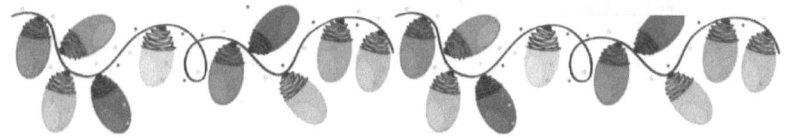

Matchmaker Christmas

Katie O'Connor

Matchmaker Christmas

Katie O'Connor

Snarky Heart Press

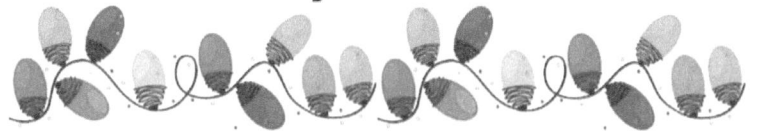

– Matchmaker Christmas –

This book is a work of fiction. Names, characters, places, and incidents either are products of the author's imagination or are used fictitiously. Any resemblance to actual events, locales, or persons, living or dead, is entirely coincidental.

Published October 2023
(katieohwrites.com)

ISBN: 978-1-989816-79-0 Digital Edition
ISBN: 978-1-989816-78-3 Print Edition

Design and cover art by P.S. Cover Designs
Editing by Terri St. Clair

Dear Santa

Santa

I want a new daddy to make mommy happy.
And a new dog and a big house.
I've been verry good this year.

Love Abby

Can Santa's Christmas magic help a single mom with a matchmaking daughter find love with a jaded billionaire?

Darcy:
Getting over my ex's betrayal has been tough and having a five-year-old daughter makes it easier and worse. Thankfully, I have a job, a home, and a mother to help us out. When my daughter enters us into The Amazing Santa Race, the last person I want to team up with is Kurt Stanwyck, my high school crush. Especially since my daughter thinks he's the dad she asked Santa for.

Kurt might just be the perfect Christmas gift. But do I want to risk getting closer and having him break my daughter's heart?

Kurt:
I've got more money than I'll ever use, but I'm bored, lonely, and there's this weird thing happening with my heart. Taking a medical sabbatical in my hometown of Salvation might just be my salvation. I'm debating leaving it all behind to work at my parent's garden center where I know I'll find the human contact I'm missing.

My folks have organized a Christmas challenge to raise money for the local hospital and they expect me to pair up with Darcy Sharp the pest who followed me around through high school. I'm not finding it as onerous as I thought I would. Darcy might just be the angel of my dreams.

How can I convince her that my money isn't an obstacle to being together and that her heart is safe with me?

Dedication

For Christmas lovers everywhere.
You know who you are, and I'm proud to be one of you.
For the Sharps and the Hecks.
Thanks for lending me your names.

Chapter One

Darcy

December first marks the start of the holiday season in my hometown of Salvation, a cozy town of only five thousand people, right on the edge of the Canadian Rocky Mountains. Salvation has been my actual salvation since my fiancé, sorry ex-fiancé, dumped me and kicked me out of our apartment when he found out I was carrying his child. He had the nerve to claim I cheated...right before he moved his secret girlfriend into our bed.

Pregnant and alone I ran home to Mom. I mean, where else is a girl gonna go when her world is blown to smithereens? Every fiber of my being hates what he's done, but I'm over him. Abby and I are better off without him. We share an apartment with Mom over her coffee shop and I have worked my way up to head cashier at the Greck's Grocery. We're doing okay. I've almost saved up enough for a downpayment on a condo or small house.

A pounding din bounces off the mall's high ceilings. I can't wait to be out of here.

"Abby, look at me." My baby girl, five years old now, bounced up and down and wiggled in her excitement to see Santa. I have to admit, he was probably the most realistic Santa I have ever seen. He sat on his sleigh in front of a screen showing snowflakes falling onto the perfect winter wonderland scene.

"Abby," I raise my voice to be heard above excited chatter of children and the overly loud Chipmunk rendition of *We Wish You a Merry Christmas*. Thank heavens the grocery store where I work prefers quiet, less shrill music. I'd never survive working in the mall for the Christmas season. The constant noise is battering my brain into mush.

"What?" Abby turned to look at me for a grand total of four seconds before turning back to the jolly man in the red suit. Her feet are in perpetual motion, jigging back and forth.

I sucked in a breath and try to chill. This is the first year she's eager to see Santa. Before now, Santa pictures featured a howling baby or frightened child. This year, she was raring to talk to him. "Abby, look at me." I grasp her shoulder and spin her around and kneel in front of her carefully keeping my much-needed coffee upright. It's just about cool enough to guzzle.

"What? I want to watch Santa. It's almost my turn. I need to give him my list."

Ah, the list. She'd been making and discarding lists since last summer. Each and every list was put through the shredder when she created a new version. I'd recently taught her the concept of privacy and was regretting it. She kept telling me I had to respect the privacy between her and Santa. I wasn't worried, but I would like an inkling of what she intended to ask for.

"Abby, remember that Christmas is about love and hope, not things. Be sure to ask for something small, okay?"

"Can I ask him for a phone?" Ugh. The phone thing. Again. *What rational parent gave a five-year-old kid their own phone?*

"You can ask but he probably won't get you one. Phones are a parent thing. Okay?" I took a deep breath. "It might be wiser to ask for something a little more reasonable. Remember, Santa brings gifts to all the children and gifts aren't free." I loved that she still believed in the magic of Christmas and hated having to remind her that money was tight. I wish I could give her everything her little heart desired. Within reason.

3

"Santa's elves make the gifts. That's free." Her grin is irresistible and I grin back.

"Either way, free or not, do not ask for a phone. Santa won't give you something I don't approve of." I tried to keep my voice firm, but her irrepressible spirit always makes me smile. She's the eternal optimist.

The sound of the Chipmunks fade as a commotion rose behind us. I pivot to look, just as two wrestling eight-year-old boys crash into us sending my coffee spiraling into the air and straight down on Abby's red and white Christmas dress.

Her scream of terror rakes down my spine like claws. The drink was hot, but not hot enough to burn, but my maternal instinct kicks in and I spin her around to unzip the dress before yanking it off. I rip off my snowman sweater and wrap her in it. Her chest is slightly pink, but not burned. Moisture wells in my eyes as tears drip down her face, off her chin.

"Are you okay? Are you hurt?" I hadn't seen any burns.

"My dress. It's destroyed," she weeps.

I saved for months to buy the dress of her dreams, now it's ruined. Coffee with cream and sugar doesn't come out, no matter how you wash it. Maybe I can over-dye the stain to from white to cream. My shoulders sag. While it's possible, it won't happen in time to see Santa today.

"It's okay, honey. We'll go home and get a clean dress and come back later." I have no idea when, I have to work in less than two hours and the lineup snakes halfway down the mall.

"No," she wails, wringing her hands like a dismayed church matron. "Santa needs to see my pretty dress." Nobody pitches a fit like a heartbroken kindergartener. She stamps her foot and splashes coffee up my legs and onto my blouse.

"You can wear your green one," I offer, knowing it won't be good enough.

"Excuse me," a deep male voice says behind me. "Is she okay?"

"She's fine. Just upset that her dress was ruined." I don't look at the man, I'm too busy hugging my daughter, and not falling into the pool of coffee at our feet. His voice is deep and sexy and sends a shiver of unusual interest across my spine despite the anxiety bettering my nerves.

"I apologize for my nephews. They will be reprimanded, and I will replace the dress."

"Hang on sweetie. I'm going to talk to the man behind me." After one last hug and a look to confirm she isn't burned, I pivot and stand in one slightly uncoordinated motion. I lurch forward but manage to keep upright.

My eyes are caught by the quality fabric of his suit and the breadth of his chest. His jaw is smooth shaven and his mouth caught somewhere between a smile and a grimace. His green eyes shine with concern.

Holy cow! I know those eyes. Kurt Stanwyck. I blink and try not to growl at him. Once upon a time, a dozen years ago, Kurt had been my ideal man. Well, boy, because at eighteen, he hadn't yet reached the amazing sexy manliness I saw before me. Holy hamburgers. He was h-o-t, hot. Scorching. A lump of something I didn't want to admit rose in my throat and my mouth went dry. An irreverent part of my mind wished I'd find Kurt in my stocking on Christmas morning.

"Darcy? Darcy Sharp? Is it really you?" His smile stole my breath.

Down girl!

He flung his arms around me and pulled me to his rock-solid chest. I pushed away.

"Kurt. Hi." I inched backward, cautious of the wet floor.

"Mama, I'm cold." Abby yanked on my hand.

"Your daughter? Let's go get her a new dress. It's our fault hers is covered in coffee." Kurt knelt beside me. "Hey there. I'm Kurt. I am so sorry about your dress. Let's take your mom to the store and get you a new dress."

My heart broke at the indecision on her face. "But Santa…"

"We'll get you a dress and come back to see Santa," Kurt offered.

"Hang on. What are you doing?" I demand. Kurt might have been the captain of the football team, but he had no right to make plans on my behalf.

"Offering to make it right. We ruined her pretty dress, I'll replace it."

More than anything, I wanted to decline his offer. This was the man who spurned me when I asked him to dance at his graduation. He'd laughed and said, "I'm meant for better things," and walked away. I still wanted to punch him in the nose.

"Come on, Darcy. I can afford it."

"Are you saying I can't?" I demanded. I couldn't but that was beside the point. How dare he judge me?

He held up his hands in mock surrender, his expression serious. "I'm not saying, or implying anything. My nephews ruined her dress and I'm offering to replace it."

"Please, Mama. I really want to see Santa in a pretty dress."

"Here are some paper towels," a teenage elf shoved them toward me. "If you want to go change, I'll give you first spot in line when you come back." The girl smiled at us. "I'm so sorry this happened." The girl glared at Kurt before getting down on hands and knees and wiping the floor. What a waste of liquid gold! We had scrambled out the door this morning and I had yet to have a single sip of life-giving coffee.

"Thank you," I said gratefully. I looked at Kurt. He appeared chagrinned and hopeful. "Fine. Let's go get a new dress." I looked at Abby. "Come on, munchkin. Mr. Stanwyck is going to get you a new dress." I thanked the elf for her help and we headed down the mall toward the discount shop at the far end.

Chapter Two

Kurt

Darcy Sharp had changed. A lot. Gone was the awkward girl I remembered from high school. She'd morphed from a kind of geeky cuteness ruined by braces to stunning, and she had curves that just didn't quit. If I had been watching my nephews instead of ogling her backside, they might not have crashed into her. I felt guilty, but at the same time I was glad for the chance to reconnect.

Getting to know more people was one of the myriad reasons I returned to Salvation. Well, that and a doctor ordered vacation. This small town had made me crazy growing up, but I'm loving the friendly atmosphere here. Darcy and her daughter strode down the mall, slightly ahead of the boys and I, almost like she didn't want to associate with us. She passed three girls' clothing stores.

"Hey, Darcy, wait." I called out. She stopped and whirled around; her dark hair flew out in a wave of shining silk practically begging me to touch it. Her hair had taunted my dreams for months after I rudely declined to dance. Okay, before that. I was a typical teenage boy back then.

"What?" Her eminently kissable lips turned down at the corners.

"What's wrong with this store?" I jabbed a thumb toward Little Princess, the shop my niece adored.

Darcy blushed. "Nothing. I just like that one." She pointed to a discount place.

I realized that she was clean and neat, but her clothing wasn't new. It wasn't threadbare, but it had seen better days, yet her daughter's dress looked like it had been brand new before the disaster. "Let's go in here. It's close and we'll get back in line with Santa sooner."

"Please, Mama." Darcy's daughter clapped in excitement. "Adrianna and Desiree get to shop here."

Her plea nearly broke my heart. "Come on, Darcy. Why not? She needs a pretty dress to see Santa." Darcy gave me a death glare but nodded.

"Abby, we can look inside. Maybe they have something on sale. We'll look, but I'm not promising a dress from here."

The little one flew into the store and I corralled the boys and hauled them inside. "Ethan and Owen, if you so much as bump a display, I'll burn your Christmas presents. Got it?" They nodded, though I doubted they were worried. "As soon as we're done in this store, you will apologize to the ladies."

10

A less enthusiastic nod followed. "Keep your hands in your pockets."

Abby raced through the store touching one dress after another.

"Abigail Morgan Sharp, do not touch the clothing. Look with your eyes, not with your hands." Instantly Abby clasped her hands behind her back and stared at the floor scuffing her feet. "Come to the back with me. Let's see what's on sale," Darcy suggested, her voice firm.

"But I like this one Mama. Can I have it, please?"

The dress was beautiful. The top was white velvet and the bottom some kind of stiff red, black, and green plaid fabric. It felt like the noisy stuff my younger sister's wedding dress was made of. The dress was topped with an adorable furry white jacket with gold trim. It was sold separately.

"Darcy, can we talk?" I knew better than to suggest getting it in front of Abby. Moms hated that. More than once I'd been smacked down by a sister for usurping her authority. We stepped a few feet to the side. Standing close enough that her soft spicy scent tickled my nose and made me want to draw her into my arms, I said, "Let her have the dress. I don't mind. It'll make me feel better for not paying attention when I was supposed to be watching the boys."

"Are they yours?" she asked.

"No!" The denial flew out too loudly. "I mean. They're my nephews. I'm single. Very single." I don't know why it was so imperative that Darcy know that I was on the market, it just was, even though before today, I wasn't on the market. "I noticed you called her by your maiden name?" I made the statement a question.

"Still single. I was engaged but that ended."

"Can she have the dress?" I asked, despite having a million questions about Darcy, her engagement, her single status, and her daughter.

Darcy closed her eyes, revealing the slightest hint of eyeshadow. With her eyes open you could barely even see it. In the brief second when they were closed, it was all I could do not to kiss her. For ten years, I regretted not taking her up on her offer of a tour around the floor at the grad dance. But back then, I'd been too cool, she'd been a bit geeky, and I had the hots for Ashly Cooper. Turns out that Ashly, the girl of my dreams, was more shrew than anything else. Our brief relationship had ended when I found her messing around with someone else.

"Well?" I asked. "Can I buy her that dress?"

"It's really expensive." Darcy nibbled her lip and I suppressed a groan.

"Darcy, have you ever heard of Green Planet Tech?"

"Yeah, who hasn't. What does that have to do with anything?"

"I'm Green Planet Tech. It's my company. I can afford the dress." Okay, I could afford to buy the dress, the store, and the chain, and probably the mall as well. I had put everything into my work for a decade and was proud of what I accomplished.

Darcy's mouth dropped open, closed again, and opened once more. "You?" She snapped her mouth shut. "Fine. We'll try the dress on. Just the dress, not the jacket."

The saleswoman helped them find the right size and Darcy led her daughter to the change rooms. They boys and I waited near the register.

"Are we almost done? I want to go home. Shopping is the dumbest thing ever." Ethan griped; his twin nodded his agreement.

"Tough cookies. We'd be finished and home by now if you boys had behaved. Your mom asked for pictures of you with Santa, and we're going to get them, even if it takes all day. And, you will apologize to Miss Sharp." I assumed she went by Miss.

Abby raced out of the dressing room and spun in a circle before us. "Do you like it, Mr.?"

"Call me Kurt. I love it. It's perfect for you. Here, try this on." He handed her the matching jacket.

Darcy glared.

"Come on, Darc. It's Christmas."

She stormed up to me until her face was inches from mine. She was about six inches shorter than I was, the perfect height, in my opinion. Her breath was minty fresh and I wanted to dive in for a taste.

"I can hardly say no now, can I? Don't ever do that again," she hissed.

"Sorry." Guilt hit me hard. I knew better but acted on impulse. I wasn't used to parenting. Well, not parenting exactly. Friending? "It won't happen again. Besides, look at her smile. She's in heaven." Abby looked sweet, happy, and adorable. Darcy's frown turned to a soft, loving smile.

"Let's pay for this and go back to Santa," I suggested. I leaned close to steal another whiff of her perfume and to whisper, "After Santa, I'll buy you guys lunch, to make up for the delay."

"No, but thanks. Let's just get these pictures over with. You've spent more than enough on us already."

Reluctantly, I agreed. I'd love to get to know Darcy again. Salvation wasn't large, only five thousand people and just the one mall. I was sure to bump into her again. I was surprised I hadn't seen her in the three weeks I'd been at home.

With a million holiday events planned, including the charity scavenger hunt, The Amazing Santa Race, arranged by my parents, I was sure to stumble on her again. The family greenhouse was hosting the event and because I was home for the holidays, I'd been rooked into helping during my forced vacation, as well as making a donation to cover expenses.

I didn't want to take the sabbatical just because I had one tiny infarction. Now, I had seeing Darcy to look forward to. Things were looking up.

Chapter Three

Darcy

While one saleswoman removed the tags from Abby's new outfit, Kurt chatted to a second clerk and paid for the clothing. His smile was a breathtaking as it had always been. With his dark hair and green eyes, he was still a heartbreaker. He'd been in and out of my mind over the years. I had often wondered how he was doing and if he were still single, not that I'd ever ask his mother.

Down girl!

I warned myself off. I didn't need a man. Abby and I were fine just the way we were. Even if she didn't agree. She was a kid, what did she know? Still, Kurt was attractive. He had just the barest hint of a shadow along his jaw. Not a five o'clock shadow, but just the hint of a scruff. My fingers itched to touch it. All that thick, amazing dark hair, and those expressive eyes, they were my Achilles heel for sure.

"You didn't need to buy her the jacket," I said as we left the store. "But I do appreciate it. You've given her the dream outfit I couldn't." I pushed as much gratitude as I could into my voice. It meant a lot that he'd been so kind after what had essentially been an accident. Accepting the beautiful dress hurt my pride, but it was generous of him.

"My pleasure. Boys, stop shoving right now." His nephews stopped nudging each other for exactly three steps. "Last warning."

His firm, authoritative voice sent shivers down my spine. What was it about a man in charge that stirred me up so much? He didn't sound angry, or mean, but there was a definite don't mess with me vibe to his tone. Firemen, police officers, Kurt…they all had a certain—yum factor.

Three minutes later, we stood in front of Santa waiting for an adorable three-year-old to finish her very long wish list. She finally hopped down, took her candy cane from the elf, and hurried to her mother's side.

"Okay, it's your turn," I said to Abby. I knelt in front of her and whispered, "Do not ask for a phone. Santa can't do that. Okay?" She nodded, but her belligerent expression said she had no intention of listening to me. I'd have to tamp this down or Christmas morning would be one big disappointment.

"I won't, Mama. I have something else I want." She waved her crumpled list.

Chapter Four

Abby

I might be only five, but I'm smart. I know this isn't the real Santa, but he looks pretty good. I think his beard is real. Adrianna and Desiree, they're my best friends, told me that mall Santa is real Santa's helper. If I give this one my list, he'll take it to real Santa.

I worked hard on my list. I changed it lots. Now, it was perfect.

"Hi, Santa," I said and climbed up on his lap. I wasn't afraid of him anymore. He was a stranger, but like the people who work in stores, he was a good stranger. That's what Mom says. She worries too much. Like about the phone. I want a phone, but I know I won't get one. It isn't fair.

"Have you been a good girl this year, Abigail?"

"How did you know my name?"

"I know everyone's names. Now, tell me what you want for Christmas this year, because I know you've been good and you've been working on that list all year long."

How did he know?

I gave him my paper. I tried not to cry because it was damp and wrinkled. It was beautiful before those stupid boys bumped Mom's coffee on me.

"You've put a lot of work into this. Your coloring has improved a lot."

He got a funny look on his face when he read my list.

"That's a big list," he said.

"Only four things. I want a daddy, a big house, a puppy, and a huge family," I tell him. "I don't even care if I don't get anything else. 'Specially if I get a new Dad. I want someone handsome for Mama and I. And he needs to have a good job so we're not poor anymore." I leaned close and whispered my terrible secret. "I don't like wearing not new stuff. I want to shop at new stores, not used ones." I hide my face cause I'm 'barrased.

"Well, Abby, life gives us things we don't always like. Being a good girl means being happy with what we have. Can you do that for me?"

"Yes!" I almost jump up because I'm so excited. Good girls get their Christmas wishes.

"Now, I can't promise anything, but Christmas is magic and I'll think very seriously about your list."

He looked at Mama and she looked upset. Santa frowned a little. I patted his cheek. "Thank you, Santa. I'll be good and I'll be happy with what you bring me."

I hop off his lap, I'm so excited I want to shout and yell. I feel like a gazillion butterflies are dancing in my tummy. The good way, not like when I need to barf.

Chapter Five

Darcy

I watched Abby race up to Santa and threw herself into his arms. "Hi, Santa." She settled onto his lap and leaned in close when he asked what she wanted for Christmas. She handed him the list she'd been clutching all day. Even from here I could see it was splattered with coffee. The man was so deep in character that he didn't even flinch at the soggy list.

Santa unfolded the colorful paper and looked at it. For a fraction of a second, his smile slipped and his gaze flashed to me. What had she asked for? I shrugged and smiled at the old guy. He winked at me and gave me a subtle thumbs up.

Kurt's voice rumbled deliciously in my ear. "What's she up to? She looks guilty."

"She has one wish I know of. A cell phone, which she's too young for. Beyond that?" I shrug. "She struggled with the list for months, but refused my help. She could have written anything."

"I gather you said no to the phone. That's going to be disappointing."

His compassionate tone was soothing to my frazzled nerves.

"What do you want for Christmas, Darcy? A new car? A hot date? A singles' cruise?"

Though he was obviously teasing, I turned to stare at him. "I am not looking for a man. I've been a single mom since I learned I was pregnant. I do not need a man." The words felt harsh so I added, "I'm not opposed to dating, but I'm not looking. Does that make sense?"

"Clear as mud." He winked and his green eyes sparkled.

Was he flirting with me? Heat rose in my face. I couldn't remember the last time a near stranger had flirted with me. Kurt wasn't exactly a stranger, but he'd been gone for years and apparently now, he had more money than Scrooge McDuck and the Kardashians combined, and that made me uncomfortable. I didn't know how to flirt on a good day, let alone above my income level, when I was covered in cold coffee. I sighed. What did it even matter? After we finished with Santa, I probably wouldn't see Kurt again.

An elf led Abby away from Santa and the jolly man waved me toward him. He shifted on the bench seat of his sleigh and patted it. Reluctantly, I sat beside him.

"Abby asked me for a dad," he said low enough that nobody else would hear.

"I'm sorry." What else could I say?

"No apologies needed. Children have minds of their own. I just thought you should know. Besides, you never know what will happen. Remember, Christmas is a time of miracles." His ho ho ho sounded genuine and not at all forced. If I closed my eyes, I'd swear he was the real deal.

"You've been a good girl this year, Darcy. I'll bring you something special this year. Keep your eyes open for those holiday miracles."

Wow! This guy really got into his role. I studied him for a second. His suit was real velvet, and his beard one hundred percent natural. He must have been growing it for months, or longer. His glasses were perfect and round and magnified his eyes. Somehow, I didn't have the heart to disagree with the old man. "I'll watch for them. Wait. How did you know my name? Did Abby tell you?"

"I know everyone's name." He winked conspiratorially. "Merry Christmas, Darcy."

"Merry Christmas, Santa." I climbed down and went to get Abby where she stood with Kurt and his nephews.

"Can I buy you lunch?" Kurt asked, obviously ignoring my previous refusal.

My heart fluttered. "No, thank you."

"Please, Mama?" Abby begged. "I like Mr. Kurt and I'm hungry." I couldn't help but wonder if her liking Kurt had anything to do with her humiliating request to Santa.

"Come on, we can go to the pizza joint in the mall. The kids can play games while we chat. They'll all love it and I'd like to spend a bit of time with you."

His serious expression surprised me. He glanced toward his nephews where they sat having an animated discussion with Santa, and then he looked down at me. "Come on, Abby. We're adults and I think we could be friends."

I knew eating with him was a bad idea. "I guess lunch would be okay." I snapped my mouth shut. Why was I agreeing to things without meaning too? First the dress, then Santa, now lunch. It was like my mind was on vacation, and my heart had taken over thinking.

"Excellent."

Before I knew what happened, I was sitting across from him in Frank's Pizza. The entire place rang with the excited shouts of children racing from game to game. Frank's was one of those kid friendly places with games you played to win tickets which could be turned into prizes. It was Abby's favorite place to eat. I avoided it at all costs. It was too loud for my tastes and the games could drain your bank account.

The air was heavy with cheese and basil. Frank's makes a great pizza. I salivated thinking about it. The noise level was deafening. Christmas music played over the banging, clanging, and ringing of games. The continual pounding on my eardrums always gave me a blistering headache. As soon as I sat down, I took some pain meds. Sort of a pre-emptive strike against the agony I knew was coming. I did not want to go to work with a headache.

"Are you okay?" Kurt asked, concern in his eyes and voice.

He was so sweet. "This place makes my head hurt, but Abby adores it." I remember all the high school gossip about how nice he was to his girlfriends. Even when they split, they remained friends with him. His kindness had been part of his appeal and apparently it still was.

"The boys do too. I thought it would nice for us to sit and chat without kids distracting us. Tell me what you've been up to since graduation."

"Just like that, you want me to sum up my life?" I laughed. "I went to college, got a job, got pregnant, came

27

home. I'm working at Greck's Grocery. I live with my mom above Ground In. She owns the coffee shop." I summed up my life as fast as I could. "What about you?"

"University for environmental engineering and then stuck around for a second degree in electrical engineering. I doubled up classes and finished both degrees in six years. In my spare time I did some work for an environmental group and founded Green Planet Tech. I did okay."

I snorted. "Okay? Dude, you're *the* name in green technology. Rumor has it that you've got almost as much money as Musk or Gates."

He laughed and everyone in the busy pizzeria turned to look and smile. The man had magnetism oozing from every pore. Was it any wonder I was smitten with him in high school?

"I did okay. I'm not in their league, but I'm not hurting either."

"What brings you back to Salvation? Are you here for the holidays?"

"I'm on sabbatical. I'm helping out my folks in the greenhouse. It's a nice break. I'm enjoying the personal interactions. I don't get much of that as a CEO." Something in his eyes told me there was more to his sabbatical than he mentioned. There was sadness in his tone and a frown darkened his eyes. Instantly, his expression brightened. "Having lunch with you is the highlight of my week so far."

Oh yeah, I'd have to watch myself around Kurt, his charm was lethal to a single woman's heart. "Flattery will get you nowhere," I warn.

He winked and I knew my words are lies. His charm could…well it could charm the pants right off a woman. I mentally slammed that door shut. Not interested.

Chapter Six

Kurt

Darcy had the most expressive face. Much more so than any woman I'd ever met. Even in high school, I'd been able to read her devastation when I refused her request. God, I'd been an idiot back then. So cocky and uncaring. Today, her seafoam green eyes were ringed with darker green, almost emerald and they sparkled with life and wariness. I made her nervous. I wondered why.

"Are you taking part in The Amazing Santa Race?" I asked, turning the conversation away from myself and to Salvation's number one holiday activity.

"We are. At least I hope we are. Abby and I are paired up with my best friend, Morgan. She's been down with the flu. I hope she's okay by Friday. Abby will be devastated if we can't participate."

"Can't just the two of you take part?"

"Groups must be at least three people for all stages and nobody can miss more than one event. If Morgan's out, Mom can't help because she's too busy, and literally everyone else I know is teamed up already. This is *the* Christmas event. It lasts all month with different challenges every three days."

"I didn't know about the teams. It wasn't like that when I was a kid."

"It's something new this year. Last year a team of fifteen cleaned house. There's a new rule that all teams are three to six people and they must work together at all times. No separations. No exceptions. There will be volunteer judges all over town."

"Well, if Morgan can't come, you should show up. I remember teams being formed last minute. Maybe you can find another person to hook up with."

I froze when the sentence slipped out of my mouth. No way did I want Darcy pairing up with anyone but me. Nope. Accustomed as I was at making snap business decisions, my instant distress at the idea of Darcy with someone else didn't worry me. I was feeling territorial towards her and didn't mind one bit.

"We might do that. Abby will be devastated if she can't participate."

The server arrived with our pizza and like metal filings to a magnet all three kids appeared out of nowhere.

Lunch passed in a wave of noise and laughter. Abby had a cute sense of humor which my nephews indulged with a continual barrage of groan-worthy dad jokes.

"How does Darth Vader like his Christmas turkey?" Owen asked.

"I don't know why?" I answered. Darcy covered her eyes, clearly knowing what was coming.

"He likes it on the dark side." I groaned and we all laughed. Abby's eyes lit with laughter. She was the most adorable girl and her face was as expressive as Darcy's.

We finished lunch and after half an hour of games, Darcy said she had to get going. We tussled verbally over the bill and in the end, I won, though only because she had leave to get Abby to the sitter's before going to work. Honestly, as I watched her walk away, I was anticipating another tussle with her. Maybe a full, adults only, date...if I could figure out how to finagle it.

Come on, Stanwyck. You're a brilliant man. You can find a way to get another date. All I had to do was put my mind to it. They boys and I headed back to Mom and Dad's farm. Mom was going to watch them while I worked in the greenhouse. My sister would be home from work in an hour or so.

Pine, spruce, and cinnamon assaulted my nose as I entered the greenhouse. Dad waved a distracted hi as he hurried past with a customer hot on his heels. I paused and let the holiday scents wash over me. Memories of my past rushed by. As a teen, I hated working here and chaffed at the continual supervision by my parents. Now, there was a quiet peace that soothed my soul. Time and perspective changed everything.

"Hi, Jake," I greeted the teenage cashier. "How's it going?"

"It's insane. Three people called in sick and we don't have anyone in the tree lot. Your dad and I are doing double duty." He groaned. It must be bad if Jake was complaining. The kid had an amazing work ethic. He had all the enthusiasm I'd lacked growing up.

"I'll bundle up and get out there. If you can handle the register," I offered. It was Saturday and it was busy. There was a line of about fifteen people at the register and dozens more swarming the aisles of holiday merchandise. They held ornaments, wreaths, wrapping papers, plants, seeds, stars made from willow branches. Many had go-cups of cocoa or cranberry apple cider. Children munched on tree shaped sugar cookies.

"Thanks, dude." Jake immediately turned his attention to the next person in line and greeted them with a smile. I'd been filling in for my folks for three weeks and Jake was always upbeat. The customers loved him. He was the employee I should have been as a teenager.

Five minutes later, I helped an elderly couple load a tree on top of their SUV. "We do have a delivery and setup service, if you are interested."

"It's okay," the old guy said. "My son will be over this afternoon to set it up, but we appreciate the offer. Thanks."

"Well, if something changes, give us a call. Wildrose Greenhouses is happy to help." As they drove away, I found myself wondering if Darcy had a tree yet. I'd ask Dad, but he'd want to know why I was curious. Plus, not everyone shopped with us or had real trees. Being nosy was harder than I anticipated.

I rushed around the greenhouse around like a chicken with my head cut off and frankly, I enjoyed every second. Even the crying kids. I missed people. Sitting in my high-rise office, day after day, I had entirely too little human interaction beyond my assistant and senior staff. Being in the thick of the early holiday rush was exhilarating and I found myself grinning for no reason.

Around three, we fell into a bit of a lull. We were open until nine on Saturdays in December, so it was certain to get busy again. I was petering out. I needed caffeine. Not Mom's delicious home brew, but a wicked, strong enough to stand on, triple expresso.

Since more staff had arrived, I left an employee in charge of the outside lot, promising him a mocha, and went inside. "Mom, I'm making a coffee run. Do you want anything?"

"A pumpkin spice latte for me, peppermint latte for your father, and can you swing by the grocery and get a loaf of bread. Ask Beverly at the coffee shop if she can spare some cocoa mix. I'm nearly out and the order won't be here until the day after tomorrow. I ran out because my cocoa is extra popular this year." Her smile was enormous.

My mother used powdered cocoa mix as the base for her famous hot chocolate. I'm not certain what she does to it in the huge vats she makes, but nobody believes it started as a mix.

I borrowed the keys to Dad's truck and raced back to town. I hit the grocery store and grabbed a loaf of whole wheat bread and another of sourdough, and headed for the register. Just as I stepped up to the conveyor, Darcy moved in and replaced the cashier.

"Darcy, hi." I almost groaned at my lame greeting. I was a suave businessman. I gave speeches to conferences around the world, and here I was tongue-tied. I put my bread on the conveyer and moved forward as it did.

"Kurt, hi," she said as she beeped my items through.

I randomly tossed on some gum and a couple chocolate bars, just to delay checking out and to give more time for conversation. She gave me my total and I whipped out my leather wallet.

"That's a nice wallet," she said. "Custom?"

I glanced down. "Yeah, my nephew made it for me in Scouts. It matches the belt his brother made me." I flashed her my stamped and dyed belt.

"It's nice that you use them." Her voice held surprise.

"Why wouldn't I? They were gifts from my nephews. I adore them." She must really think I was shallow. Ouch. I'd have to prove her wrong. "Remind me to show you the scarf my niece knit for me." I tapped my card as she bagged my bread in a paper sack. Greck's was old school. They'd never adopted the use of plastic instead sticking with paper bags. I admired that. Paper was easy to reuse and recycle. It was sustainable, unlike plastic. Mom reused her personal grocery bags in the greenhouse to wrap plants and bag items.

I glanced around before I spoke, I didn't want to embarrass Darcy. Salvation was a small town and gossip travelled fast. "Can I buy you dinner sometime?"

She blushed adorably. "Um. Maybe?" She winced.

"No pressure." I scratched my cell number on a business card and handed it to her. "Think about it. Call me when you decide." I smiled broadly and winked before picking up my bag and leaving. At the door, I turned back to find her staring after me. Nice to know I made an impression on her; I just hoped it was a good one. I gave her a nod of acknowledgement and headed to the coffee shop.

"Kurt Stanwyck, as I live and breathe," Darcy's mom, Beverly, raced from behind the order counter and threw her arms around me. "It's been years. You look great." Once upon a time, I'd done deliveries for the grocery store and often dropped off small orders for Darcy's mom.

"Hi, Mrs. Sharp. Good to see you."

She patted my back. "Don't be so formal, call me Beverly." She took my hand and tugged me forward. "What can I get you?"

"Mom needs to borrow some cocoa mix until next week and I've got a drink order a mile long." She waggled her fingers and I passed over the list. She immediately handed it to the teenage girl behind the counter.

I did a double-take. "Aren't you Santa's elf?"

"Aren't you the hero who bought Abby a new dress?" she countered.

"Guilty as charged."

"That was you?" Mrs. Sharp gushed. "Abby is so proud of that dress. She won't take it off. Come see." She waved me into the kitchen where Abby stood on a chair beside a middle-aged man in a white chef's jacket.

"Abby, come say thank you to Mr. Stanwyck for your new dress."

She whirled around, nearly toppling off her chair.

"Mr. Kurt! Thank you for my new dress. I love it. I'm even 'tecting it." She stroked the adorable mini-apron that covered her dress. "I don't want to get it messy."

"Great way to protect it." She was adorable, she had Darcy's smile and laughing eyes.

"Kurt, can you grab the cocoa for me? It's on the top shelf." Beverly showed me where to find it and I lifted it down. She was a tiny bit of a woman and there was no way she'd lift twenty pounds of cocoa mix from the top storage shelf without a ladder.

"Mrs. Sharp, Beverly, do you have a Christmas tree yet?"

"No, dear. I'll just set up my artificial one again."

"Mom said you get a free tree for getting her out of a bind with the cocoa. Did you want to bring Darcy and Abby out to pick one tonight? No charge. We'll even deliver." I threw the idea out without thinking. I wanted to see where Darcy lived. If I gave them a tree, I would pay for it, and deliver it, then I'd get a peek into her life. I found that I was insatiably curious about grownup Darcy Sharp.

"A fresh tree would be lovely, and very much appreciated but tonight doesn't work well. How about we pick something tomorrow after the race launches? Would that work."

"Perfectly. It's a date. I'll see you after the launch." We made small talk while my drinks were finished. I paid and raced back to work. My heart thumped in anticipation. It felt good, unlike the intermittent pounding when I had my 'incident.'

Chapter Seven

Darcy

I couldn't believe it; Morgan was still sick. What she thought was food poisoning or mild flu turned out to be a severe viral stomach bug. It seemed like half the town had it. Now, I'm hoping Abby doesn't pitch a fit if we aren't able to compete this year. It's the first year she's been old enough to be an official participant and not just follow along with our group. There's no way Mom can help out, she's just too busy this time of year.

Abby and I dress warmly and pack a bag of snacks and drinks. Today's task could be outdoors, or a long day, if we managed to find someone to team up with. I liked to be prepared for anything.

The greenhouse parking lot is jammed. No room left room to park. Lucky for me, I know there's a staff lot in the back. I sneak around the back and slide my small Toyota into a space so tight I almost had to climb out my window.

Inside, we join everyone in one of the greenhouses that have been emptied of merchandise for the event, and I let

Mr. Stanwyck know I cheated and parked out back. The room smelled of cinnamon, cocoa, and evergreen. Wreaths and swags made from fresh greenery hung from the walls and rafters. It reminded me of Christmas as a kid. My heart swelled with joy. Peace washed over me. However, the day went, it would be okay. I would make it a great day for Abby.

Around us, everyone is clustered in small groups, I don't see any loners or two-person groups besides Abby and I. Just as I kneel to remind her we might not get to participate, a microphone crackled. I turn my attention to the stage and nearly trip over my tongue.

Kurt is up there and he's dressed in snow pants and a tight turtleneck in the most amazing shade of teal. Holy Hanna, he's delish. He begins his introduction and welcome speech, and his voice tickles over me like heat from a fireplace. He talks for a few minutes and winds up everything by saying, "If there is anyone here who needs another group member, please come forward. If there is a group that wouldn't mind an extra member, let us know, maybe we can help some of the less fortune players out. This is a great chance to get to know your neighbors."

A lone woman was paired with a couple and their young child. Two groups of two were blended. That left only Abby and I unmatched. I searched the room, praying for someone, anyone to step up for us. Two of the families from her class at school had room for us but looked away every time I tried to catch their eye. I tried not to be disappointed by their snub.

"Come on, people? We've got a mom and her little girl who are dying to compete. Anyone willing to step up?" The crowd fell dead silent. "Okay, then," Kurt said slowly. "Is there any objection to me teaming up with them? I don't run this event; I didn't help plan it. I'm just the pretty face on stage." He winked outrageously and the crowd laughed as he obviously meant them too.

"You don't have to do that," I called out, humiliation burning my cheeks.

"Yay, Mr. Kurt," Abby squealed.

"Any objections? Speak now or forever hold your peace. Once I sign up, the organizers won't take any complaints on me teaming up with this small family." His gaze searched the crowd.

"Oh, for the love of Pete, just sign up already. I'm sweating to death in this snow suit," a man called. He had a point; Abby and I had taken off our jackets ten minutes earlier. It was roasting.

"Okay then. I'll go complete my paperwork and my father will fill us in on the first task." He handed his father the mic and hopped off the stage landing right at our feet in a superhero pose making Abby giggle. "Come on ladies, let's go add me to your roster."

While Kurt filled in the paperwork, I listened to the day's instructions. Today's event was an actual scavenger hunt. Each team was given list of twenty things to find. No two teams had the same items. This was to ensure there was no cheating, and to prevent one team from stealing another team's item. The first team to report back with all their items was declared the winner and received the most points.

Each list came in a sealed envelope. Kurt's father hollered, "On your marks, get set, go!" The crowd rumbled with excitement as we tore into the envelopes. "Remember to stay together at all times. No splitting up."

44

I scanned the list. It was designed to get participants into local businesses and attractions. There were several simple items, like a jelly donut from Bill's Bakery and a mochaccino from Mom's shop. These items would be given to us without charge. Some items seemed impossible, like the key to the city. As if that were an actual thing.

"Let's do the hard ones first. If we pass an easy one on the way, we'll grab it," I decided aloud. "We'll take my car; we can scoot out the back exit. Abby, you hold the list. Careful not to lose it."

I fumbled with my keys and dropped them twice while trying to unlock the car. What I wouldn't give for a car with keyless entry or one of those touch pad things.

Kurt said, "Let me get that," and hurried around to my side.

I passed him the keys and he immediately dropped them. "Candy canes," he growled.

We dropped to our knees, smacking heads on the way down. I tried to scoot back out of his way and my legs shifted sharply left and slid under the car. I squealed and Abby laughed.

Kurt reached out to take my hand but I couldn't get back on my feet, or even my knees. I was stuck on my backside, half under the car. I realized that I was sitting on a snow dusted frozen puddle about ten feet wide. It's a wonder I hadn't fallen on my backside getting out of the car when we arrived.

"You're going to have to pull me out," I grumbled, mortification heating my cheeks. I was under the car to my waist. I lay back and stretched my arms over my head. Luckily the car that had been in the space beside me was gone and there was plenty of room.

Kurt let Abby into the other side of the car and picked his way carefully back over the ice, grumbling about how he was going to have a word with his father about snow removal. He didn't sound angry. In fact, he sounded somewhat amused. I think he found my predicament funny.

He stood over me and grinned down at me. "Need some help, princess?"

"Funny. Very funny." I swatted at his knees with my hands. He grabbed them in his, he was scalding hot against my snow-covered palms. Heat rushed through me and my heart tripped a happy beat.

"On three. One. Two. Three." He tugged gently and slowly I slid out from under the car.

We climbed in and drove back toward town and straight for the mayor's office. If the key to the city existed, the mayor would have it.

Oddly, the office was open today. Usually, it was only open Monday to Friday. Inside, I recognized several other contestants. One group was headed toward the library at the other end of the building. The second group was headed into the planning department office. We waited in line until it was our turn to talk to the mayor's assistant. Why did every city hall I've ever been in smell like lemon and dust? The scent stole the joy from the beautiful Christmas decorations. The office was bedecked in red and silver. Shining stars hung from the walls and ceiling.

Instrumental holiday classics played on the overhead speakers with just enough crackle to be distracting. Our last mayor had commissioned a new town office which was beautiful on the outside but full of shortcuts, like crappy speakers, on the inside. She'd been fired when the town realized she'd cut corners and funneled the money into her own bank account.

"Hi, Gilda," I greeted my old high school friend. "I, we, need to see the mayor."

"I can schedule you an appointment for next week. He's in the city for a conference on green technology."

I resisted an unfamiliar urge to cuss. I never was much of a cusser, but quit entirely when I got my life back together before Abby came along. "I need the key to the city. Show her," I told Abby, who pushed the now wrinkled list at Gilda.

"Oh, shoot! He must have forgotten about the game." She frowned. "I'm only here because I had some paperwork to finish. I don't know if I can just give out the key without permission."

"I'll give the town of Salvation a free eco assessment," Kurt blurted. "But only if you give us the key. I'll leave my driver's license and credit card as collateral."

She seemed undecided.

"Please. We went to school together. You can trust me." I wasn't above begging and I clutched my hands together prayer-like. "Besides, the mayor must have authorized it or it wouldn't be on our list."

"I suppose so. But if I get fired, you owe me a job," she told Kurt.

"Deal."

"Yay!" Abby cheered, clapping her hands.

Gilda grabbed a set of keys and went through a doorway behind her desk. She was back in three minutes toting a six-foot-long gold key. It looked like an antique skeleton key.

"Holy snickerdoodles." Kurt laughed.

She passed me the key. It wasn't nearly as heavy as it looked. It probably weighed six or seven pounds. I'm guessing painted aluminum tubing.

"Thanks, Gilda." We raced toward the car. The key was just big enough to be awkward, but I refused to let Kurt carry it. After my disaster at the car, I needed to redeem myself. "What's next, Abby?" I asked as we piled back into the car.

"Fr-fr-frank-franklin," she stumbled her way through the unfamiliar name. "R-r-r. Oh, I can't read it. It's a big R word. Then socks." Abby muttered.

"Franklin Rosevelt's socks," I told them having read the list earlier.

"What?" Kurt squawked.

I laughed at his pique. "Franklin Rosevelt is a senior in The Pines." I headed for our local live-in senior's center.

"We have to get some old guy's socks? Gross." Kurt said while Abby made gagging sounds.

My laughter rang out way to loudly. "Pretty sure Frank knows we're coming." I giggled.

"My parents are sick people," Kurt grumbled, but I could hear the laughter in his voice.

I swatted his arm. "Come on, this is fun. Drive."

Franklin's socks were clean and neat. They didn't even have any holes. We had to get a flag from the mini-golf course, an apple from the grocery store without stealing it, or paying for it, or asking someone we knew to buy it. It took ten minutes to talk a stranger into paying for us. Jenny Burk's cat's collar was easy, as were the donut and coffee. A couple more and we were down to one item and I was at my wits' end. Where in the world were we going to find a six-inch plastic spider?

I shuddered just thinking of spiders. They were on my heck-no list. I avoided them at all costs, even the fake ones. "Okay, where do you suggest we go to find this spider." My distaste must have shown in my voice.

"Are you afraid of spiders?" Kurt asked.

"No."

"Yes," Abby piped in. "She screams like a girl."

Kurt roared at the comment.

"In the summer I had to save her from a daddy long leg." My daughter's laughter was infectious.

"Interesting," Kurt steeples his fingers together and laughed evilly.

"Do not even think about it," I warned. He had no idea how freaked out I actually get. "Where should we look?"

"At the school?" Abby suggested Billy Minor had one in class last year. Mrs. Abrams took it away."

"Good idea, but the school is closed on the weekend."

"Okay," Kurt said logically. "They wouldn't ask for one unless they knew one was readily available. "One of the local stores, maybe?"

"They sell toys at Twice as Nice." Abby mentioned the church's charity shop. We headed right over. Like every other store in town, it was packed with out of towners. The Amazing Santa Race was great for local businesses and tourism.

"Let's split up and look," Kurt suggested. "You two hit toys and games, I'll look in other places, like dishes and books. I don't expect it will be where one would expect to find it."

He was right. We searched the toy department and pulled out three dozen puzzles and looked behind them. "Where to now?" I asked Abby.

"Maybe Christmas?"

"Brilliant." We bumped into Kurt on our way to the seasonal section. He had also failed out.

A creative sales associate had hung a long line of stockings on the front of a shelf housing glass and ceramic ornaments. "In the stocking," Abby shouted and started feeling them one by one. We let her look. This race was more about her than either of us.

"Oh, there's something hard in here," she said excitedly. She popped up on the tips of her toes but couldn't get her hand inside the bedazzled stocking. "Mom, you get it."

"Not me!" I waved my hands in a no-way gesture. "Kurt, you do it.'

Laughing, he dug into the stocking and pulled out a giant spider. He waved it triumphantly and stalked towards me, spider stuck out in front.

"Do not!" I warned. Abby giggled. Kurt laughed.

"Should I?" he asked her.

"Yes! No! Mama will get mad. You better not."

"Okay, you're the boss," he told her. Her grin was a mile wide.

"That's the last thing," she exclaimed, waving the wrinkled list in the air. "We need to get back before everyone else does. She grabbed Kurt's hand and yanked him toward me. Dragging us behind her, she stormed toward the checkout counter.

She must have bumped a shelf as she went because all of a sudden, a fuzzy Santa Claus fell forward right into my face. I screamed and jumped back. My damp boots were slippery and I scrambled to stay upright. No such luck.

My arms pinwheeled as I slid back and sideways knocking an entire display of stuffed animals off the shelf on top of me. I was buried and a furry landslide. Abby and Kurt laughed until they had to clutch their sides. Only when they calmed down did Kurt ask if I was okay.

"I'm fine." I admit, I was grumpy.

"Let me help you up." He unburied me and offered his hand. We restacked the toys.

"I don't know where this lack of coordination came from. I'm never unsteady on my feet," I grumble. "I do yoga and agility classes twice a week." Ya, I was bragging to impress the boy who had refused to dance with me. "I even took hip hop classes."

"Maybe I've just swept you off your feet today." Kurt's smile was slow and sensuous. It stirred something hot and needy inside me.

Chapter Eight

Kurt

Sunday's quest took four hours. I hadn't planned to spend so much time helping Darcy and Abby, but it was the most fun I've had in years. Darcy had a gift for making people feel at ease. Even me.

What I was fast coming to adore about her was her easy laughter. She even laughed at her own foibles and didn't get too upset when Abby and I teased her about landing on her backside twice in the same day. She must have thanked me fifty times for offering an eco-evaluation to get the key to the city, even though I'm pretty sure Gilda would have given it to us anyway. All my offer would cost was a few hours, maybe a couple days of my time and the town would benefit. Who knows, maybe they'd even purchase some of my green tech. If not, watching the smiles on Abby and Darcy's face when we acquired the key was worth it.

I'd shocked myself by signing up. Usually, this type of frivolity was not my thing, but here I was, two days later, standing in the doorway to the transformed greenhouse eagerly searching rows of tables and chairs for my partners.

Last night, after we closed up shop, the staff had gathered together to transform the empty greenhouse into a banquet hall of sorts. Because I was a contestant and shouldn't have unfair advantage, I'd been sent home to watch the boys. Now, the greenhouse held a barbecue and a table and chairs for each team. It was an inspirational idea because the roof of the greenhouse was rolled fully back and the room was basically outside but still surrounded by walls to cut the cold wind. Today was warmer, probably minus ten Celsius, but it was windy.

I knew from talking to Dad over breakfast, that five teams had dropped out after the first event. Some had the flu, others simply quit for reasons unsaid. I suspect that like me, they didn't realize how much time this would entail. There were ninety-five groups remaining. I was astounded at how many people took part.

Motion at the far end of the hall attracted my attention. Abby stood on a chair waving while Darcy paced back and forth. She wore the cutest frilly poinsettia apron. I quick-stepped their way. More excited to see them than I should be.

Darcy frowned at me. "You're late."

I checked my watch. "I'm exactly on time. Besides, I was with Dad and he couldn't start because he was with me." I laughed as her face morphed from the frown, to puzzlement, to relief. She had the most expressive eyes and brows. She always could convey an entire conversation without a word. I remember when I refused that dance in high school. She stood straight and tall and pretended to be unaffected. There were no tears in her eyes, but her pain showed in her brows and hit me like a sucker-punch to the nards. It gave me nightmares for weeks.

Over the years I'd dated many women, but none with a face as mobile and expressive as Darcy's. In fact, I frequently wished they'd shown more of what they were thinking. I swear some of them had been botoxed until they couldn't blink.

"What's the challenge?" Darcy asked clearly hoping for insider information which I didn't have. "Why did they ask us to bring aprons?" She handed me a matching apron with entirely too many ruffles. I draped it around my neck and tied it up with a mental groan. I probably looked like I was wearing a poinsettia dress.

"No idea what the challenge is. But I expect we'll be cooking something on these barbecues." Mom took the stage and called out a greeting.

"Look around people," she said. "You'll notice ten judges wearing red elf suits, complete with striped socks, and bells on their shoes," Mom announced and the elves hopped up on chairs and waved just as Abby had done moments ago. "They'll be watching for violations of the rules." She went on to explain the contest.

"Bake a cake on a barbecue?" Darcy glared at me like I was to blame. "I can't bake in an oven."

"Lucky for you, I love to bake." Her relieved grin made me feel like Captain America, or his Canadian cohort...whoever that might be.

We were given three recipes to choose from and a box of ingredients. There was a veritable grocery store at the side where extras were available, and a news crew walked around taking videos of everyone.

"Wait," Darcy's frown was back. "You said you couldn't cook."

"I can read a recipe, if I must. But baking is not cooking. Baking is more like a science project. Precise measurements and times. Preparing meat and veggies is considerably more variable and prone to errors. Cake I can handle. What recipes did we get?" She scanned our sheet.

I was going to open our supplies while she read, but I was transfixed by her expression. Her eyes floated left and right and back again as she flipped through the pages. Her eyes pinched tight together and then went wide. Her lips pursed together and I was struck by an almost irresistible urge to kiss her. "Peppermint cream, gingerbread spice, or devil's food cake."

We discussed our three options and went with a twist on the gingerbread spice cake, topped with cream cheese frosting. I leaned close, more to catch a whiff of her unique scent and feel the heat of her body than to keep my words a secret. "Let's give this a twist. Spice cake jelly roll with cream cheese frosting all nestled on a bed of cinnamon spiced apples."

"We don't have the pan for that." She gestured to the pile of standard cake rounds and square pans.

"That I can fix with tinfoil. Abby, can you go get four apples, this big." I showed her with my hands. "Nice ripe red ones." We'd be able to watch her from where we stood and I wanted her to feel included.

"Can I, Mama. Please?"

"Sure thing. Watch out for other people."

"It was nice of you to include her."

Darcy's praise filled me with a sense of pride almost as big as when I snagged my first corporate contract. I wanted to impress her. Even without that desire, I wouldn't leave a team member out of an event.

"We've got a veggie peeler. I thought you and Abby could peel the apples while I get started on mixing the batter and pre-heating the barbecue. Since you said you can't bake, I thought I'd run this show."

"Thank heavens!" I bit back a grin because her relief was so dramatic.

Abby picked up a small basket and started putting apples in it. She reached a bit high and elbowed an apple. It thunked to the floor. Darcy gasped and rushed toward her just as the entire pile avalanched down onto the cement floor.

I hurried to their side and started picking up the fruit. I'd put up eight or ten apples and they'd tumble back down. The lip on the shelf was too low to hold them unless they were perfectly placed. We didn't have time to waste on apple stacking, but we kept at it. I stacked and Darcy grabbed the ones that fell before they could hit the floor again. They'd all be bruised.

Mom would be busy making pies for the women's shelter and senior's center all week rather than let a few bruised apples go to waste. Eventually, with the help of a couple elves, we got the apple avalanche under control.

Darcy wasn't much better with a paring knife than Abby was with a peeler. The two were hilarious. "I thought you could cook?"

"I can. But this knife is so much sharper than Mom's knives. I'm worried I'll cut myself."

"The greenhouse has a sharpening service. Bring your mom's knives out and I'll have them tuned up for you...before someone gets hurt. Dull knives are dangerous because the dull blade resists doing what you're trying to accomplish."

I created a long flat pan with low edges from several layers of tinfoil. With luck, it would hold up under the weight of the batter until it was cooked. I opened the barbecue lid and placed the empty pan. Quickly and carefully, I spread the batter over the tray.

"Spatula," I called.

"What are you, a surgeon?" Darcy quipped and slapped the spatula handle into my waiting palm.

"Pretty close." My laughter ended when the batter starting flowing onto the heat source when my makeshift pan bent. I dropped the plastic mixing bowl splattering the remaining batter everywhere. The spatula landed with a sick wet sound as I clutched the dripping tray to keep it flat. The heat of the barbecue was killing my hands. I could almost feel my hairs burning away. Oven mitts might have been a good idea.

"Grab those skewers," I ordered, not meaning to bark.

Darcy whirled around and snatched them out of the box and slid them perpendicular to the grill and under the ends of the pan. I'd have to watch that they didn't catch fire, but they'd hold our cake upright for the short baking time, less than fifteen minutes at this temperature.

"Whew!" I exclaimed and Darcy chuckled.

"That was almost a bizaster," Abby said seriously. "Be careful," she warned me with a shake of her finger.

"I wonder where she gets that move?" I whisper in Darcy's ear. I was rewarded with a sharp elbow to the ribs.

Darcy had batter spattered all over her jeans and apron. I was worse. Batter dripped off my legs in clumps. Abby was the only one to be spared. I swiped at Darcy's jeans with a chunk of paper towel.

"Hi. Tom Stanton, station nine news. Got a minute?" We turned in unison to face the voice. Tom had been in my grade in high school. He'd always been smug and superior; claiming he'd bet a Nobel Prize in journalism.

"Sure," Darcy said.

"I notice that your aprons say, Ground In."

"They sure do," she said proudly. "My family owns the shop."

"Isn't it a conflict of interest to participate in something your family contributes to? They are one of the event's major donors."

"How is it a conflict? The organizers ask for donations and we give them. We don't plan the events or determine who gets the prizes."

I stayed out of the conversation because I was trying to stay somewhat under the wire. I was wealthy enough that people loved to track my location and what I was doing. I didn't want my presence to take away from Darcy and Abby's fun, or from the event itself which raised money for local charities.

"It seems..." he paused dramatically, "suspect to me." I heard the gloating smile in the reporter's voice and confronted him.

"Don't be ridiculous. This is a small town. Everyone knows everyone and you can rest assured that if there was any *suspect* activity, it wouldn't go unnoticed." I didn't mean to snap at him, but he was a pushy jerk, just like he'd been in high school.

"Right," Stanton drew the word into two sneering syllables. "This coming from a billionaire who has abandoned his company to cheat at a holiday contest run by his family."

I clenched my fists and counted to ten. "First off, all the participants had the right to veto me, *before* I entered. I entered to give this little Abby a chance to compete when their third partner came down with a serious illness." I forced myself to relax. "Second, my second in command is more than capable of running Green Planet Tech in my absence and will continue to do so when I retire."

I slung my arm around Darcy's shoulders. "We're old friends, as you well know, competing in a charity event. Stop trying to sully it to make headlines." I gave his cameraman a significant look and the recording light on the camera shut down before he nodded at me. I leaned in to Stanton. "Stay out of my face, and if I hear that you went anywhere near Darcy and her daughter, you'll be hearing from my lawyers."

Stanton's glare was supposed to be intimidating, I knew his type, and I knew he'd report on my being here. So much for keeping a low profile. We locked eyes until he backed away. I put him out of my mind for the time being.

The elf judges strolled around and my parents toured through, greeting everyone and making idle chitchat without being too distracting.

"Darcy, how are you?" My mom asked with entirely too much enthusiasm.

"I'm good Mrs. Stanhope. Thanks for asking. We're really having fun this year. Aren't we Abby?"

"I love baking!" Abby wiggled on the chair she knelt on. I swear the girl was in constant motion. She reminded me of a happy puppy.

"That's fabulous. Why don't you both come to dinner on Saturday? Bring your mother. We'll have a party."

I glared at Mom. What was she up to? Why was she suddenly asking random people to dinner? Not that I minded, I'd love more time with Darcy, but this smelled of matchmaking and I did not need anyone fixing me up, least of all my mother. If I needed dating help, I'd hire a professional.

Still, I was looking forward to that dinner.

Chapter Nine

Darcy

I was not looking forward to this. I glanced over at Mom as I drove past the long rows of greenhouses to the Stanwyck's home. The white trimmed, forest green bungalow sat behind their rows of greenhouses with a thick band of trees between it and whatever else they grew or did on their farm. The place was beautiful and Mom's smile matched.

"You look happy," I commented.

"I haven't spent time with Ray and Audrey in years. We used to be quite close. I'm going to enjoy catching up."

I was thrilled for her, but still worried about Abby. What if she got bored and kicked up a fuss? I should have hired a babysitter and left her at home. Too bad Mrs. Stanwyck had specifically invited her by name. I was nervous too. It had taken a week to find a mutually workable date for this dinner and I'd spent entirely too much time with Kurt. As an adult, he was even more enticing than he had been as a boy. I didn't realize it back then, but Kurt was nothing like the man he'd matured into. I had been smitten by the boy and fast falling under the man's spell. Too bad he was only here temporarily because I could see us dating. Seriously dating.

Now I was spending even more time with him and further risking my heart. I swallowed my sigh lest Mom hear it and start pestering me. She had an uncanny way of knowing what I was thinking. I did not want her digging around inside my head. She was good about nagging me to date, but sometimes she couldn't help herself.

Someone was sitting on a swing in the shade of the trees out front of the Stanwyck's house when we pulled up. I slipped the car into park and climbed out. Kurt strode out of the trees with a huge smile on his face. "I thought you weren't coming after all. I'm glad you made it." He greeted Mom and Abby and held Abby's hand as he led us inside.

Inside was chaos. The twins from the mall and a girl Abby's age raced around in some complex game only kids understood. "Hi, Jenny," Mom called as the girl raced by.

Jenny stopped and grabbed Abby's hand. "Come on." Abby kicked off her shoes and joined in their game. We followed Kurt to the kitchen.

"Mrs. Stanwyck, thanks for having us." She rushed to my side and hugged me, and then Mom.

"I've waited too long. I meant to invite you when you first moved back. I can't believe it's been almost six years. Time just seems to roll away sometimes. I'm glad we're finally together, and please, call me Audrey."

Mrs. Stanwyck had always been super enthusiastic, happy, and outgoing. She was practically a force of nature. Her husband, Ray, was just as bad only he tended to slip into the background in large groups. Tonight, he came right over and struck up a conversation.

Kurt's brother and two sisters were deep in a whispered conversation in the corner near the back door. They broke off almost immediately when we entered. I would have liked more time to study the bright sunny kitchen and the view out back, but before I knew it, we were hustled to the table.

We gathered in an enormous extension to the kitchen. The walls were freshly painted but the baseboards and trim were only partially finished. The oval kitchen table was set for the kids, and sawhorses held up what I suspected were old doors to seat the adults. The makeshift table was covered with a white linen cloth.

"Sorry the room isn't finished, we're renovating. Eventually, I'll find the right table for this space." Audrey waved us forward.

Kurt sat beside me. The table was large but not quite big enough. Kurt's knee kept brushing mine. I'd worn an above the knee skirt and stockings and the heat of his leg burned into me. I kept shifting away, but every time I relaxed, we touched again. Concentrating on the delicious dinner was almost impossible.

Audrey sat on my left and we chatted easily. Owen came between us and tugged on Audrey's arm. "Grandma. I need more gravy." He thrust his plate toward her. It tipped ominously and she made a grab for it.

The plate cartwheeled through the air toward me. It landed with a gross splat and a crack on the table between Kurt and I. Owen burst into tears. "My dinner," he wailed.

"My shirt," Kurt grumbled under his breath.

I dabbed at the mashed potatoes and the broccoli bits covered in cheese that littered my silk blouse. It was probably ruined. I knew better than to wear my good clothing near children but I wanted to look nice.

Owen's mom, Gena, and Audrey, jumped up to mitigate the disaster. A flurry of activity ensued with too much chatter, tears, and wiping up. I wanted to cry, and I wanted to laugh.

Back in high school, I'd been geeky and uncoordinated. I'd grown out of that phase long before Abby arrived. Since I'd bumped into Kurt again, I was thrust back into that awkward phase. I'd tripped, fallen, stumbled, spilled, been spilled on...oh, and don't forget the apple disaster. My life was turning into a slapstick comedy.

Gena led me to a bedroom at the back of the house and found me something to wear. She swore up and down that she'd replace my shirt if it didn't come clean.

"Don't be silly. It's just a shirt and the spill was an accident," I said as we started back to the kitchen.

"Actually," Kurt's voice startled me as he came out of an adjacent bedroom. "It was as much Mom's fault as it was anyone else's. I'll have the shirt replaced for you."

I stopped mid-stride, hands on my hips. Gena gave us a side look and disappeared down the hallway, leaving us alone. "You will not."

"Yes, I will. My family invited you to dinner and we ruined a lovely blouse. I'll replace it."

First Abby's dress. Now my blouse. It seemed like Kurt was trying to be us entire new wardrobes. Okay, that was an exaggeration, but somehow his kindness just seemed to emphasize the financial differences between us and it left me feeling...inadequate somehow. I had almost managed to forget about his money, until that reporter showed a microphone in my face. Now, this whole blouse thing...it was giving me a stomach ache.

"Fine, I'll buy myself a new blouse and send you the bill," I lied.

"You do know that I can see the lie on your face. Your face is incapable of keeping a secret." He stroked a finger down my cheek. "Darcy, there's no shame in struggling to get by. Let me do this for you."

His touch was soft and warm. He was close enough that his breath was like a butterfly's wing against my cheek. My eyes drifted shut. Blouse forgotten, I battled the temptation to lift up on my toes and kiss him. I'd dreamed of kissing Kurt since I was sixteen.

Not happening.

"How about we discuss this later?" I said, backing away. "Let's just finish dinner."

His stare was penetrating, like he could read my every thought. Did he know how much I wanted to kiss him. I looked down at the floor, hiding my eyes from him.

"Oh, Darcy," he murmured. "What am I going to do with you?"

My heart and mind screamed delicious ideas at me and I pinched my lips shut, opening them only enough to say, "Nothing. Nothing at all."

Chapter Ten

Darcy

I survived the dinner. Barely. My body was so attuned to Kurt that I was aware of every breath he took. It simultaneously dragged on and sped by way too fast. I was relieved to get out of there and go home. I haven't slept well since. I didn't see him yesterday, but it was Tuesday again and The Amazing Santa Race continued. We were holding our own, but could easily fall behind. With events on Tuesdays, Thursdays, Saturdays, and Sundays we were keeping busy. The winning team would be announced at the tree trimming on the solstice.

With all the time required, Kurt was making an enormous time commitment to keep my daughter happy. Today's event was the toboggan challenge. Almost everyone who participated went to Slippery Slopes to cheer the others on. Highlights were streamed on Salvation's social media accounts. The streaming had started three years ago and every year, there were more and more tourists taking part.

I don't understand how people can afford to live in a strange place for nearly a month, but it was good for Salvation's bottom line.

Everyone was assigned a time to be at the hill. Each team had to climb up the steep and slippery left side of the hill and then toboggan down the right. Scoring was based on time with time added for non-completion.

The Slopes' parking lot was full and there was a line of food trucks serving virtually everything including venison kabobs, corndogs, smokies, pizza and burgers. A huge bonfire burned near the base of the hill and Christmas music blared over speakers hung from the parking lot lights. Down the road about a hundred yards, there was a petting zoo that included reindeer.

"Holy Christmas," Kurt exclaimed getting out of his SUV. "This is nuts."

I laughed. "It's always like this. Every event has a crowd. The whole town gets into the spirit of the games even if they aren't competing."

"I had no idea."

"How long has it been since you were home for this?"

"Ten years. Mom said it had grown, but wow!"

I couldn't stop a giggle at his astonishment. "I hope you work out," I teased. "This is a tough test." The air was frosty and still. Thankfully there was no breeze to steal our heat. The sun peeked between clouds making the snow glitter and shine like a crystal wonderland.

We watched three burly men jog to the top of the hill and barrel down on the sled they were provided. They came in at under three minutes.

"How is that fair?" Kurt grumbled. "We've got a kid."

I laughed. "It works out. Later, there's an event where you have to climb through a narrow tube. None of them will even fit into it and they'll have to take a forfeit. There are even considerations for teams with members with mobility issues." I pointed to a young man in a wheelchair. "Didn't you read the rules?"

"Why would I? I'm home for Christmas, I didn't actually come to compete. Maybe I should read them tonight so I know what I'm up against."

"Good plan."

One group took a forfeit for being unable to get to the top in the required time. One dropped out altogether. A third group fell of their toboggan. Because none of them made it to the bottom on the sled, they took a forfeit as well. Two groups sprinted up the hill as easily as if they were walking down the street. I knew them from the local ski patrol. They had mad mountain skills and were used to working in the snow. Abby and I had tobogganed here two weeks ago and I knew the climb was brutally slippery. "We're doomed."

"I'll carry Abby up the hill, we'll make better time that way."

"Nope. Everyone has to reach the top on their own steam. We can help, but we can't carry her. And, at least one member must stay on the sled all the way to the bottom."

Before he could reply, our number was called and we were lining up at the bottom of the hill. The judge recapped the rules and we were off. The hill was as slippery as I expected, but not dangerously so. Kurt took three long strides and reached back to help Abby over a hump. He held her steady as she scrambled up toward the small ledge he stood on. When she was stable, I reached for his hand. I'd taken no more than two steps when I felt myself tipping backwards, head-over-heels. I lashed out with my other hand, trying to grab him. In what felt like slow motion, I cartwheeled over and over, back down the hill. I hit the bottom with a grunt as a thousand pounds of man landed on top of me. I was getting tired of looking like a fool in front of Kurt.

Icy snow chilled my neck where it seeped between my hat and scarf. I shivered. My back was cold but my front was heating rapidly. Okay, maybe this wasn't all bad.

"Are you okay?" Kurt groaned.

I took mental stock. I could barely breathe, but nothing seemed broken. "Yeah," I grunted. "I think so." He'd lost his hat somewhere and his hair was all askew, like he'd just woken up. Wouldn't I like to be the lucky lady who woke up beside him every day? I stared up into his mesmerizing green eyes.

Kurt stared back at me. He didn't move a single muscle. We just stared. For a moment, I thought I saw the future flash before my eyes. Then I heard Abby calling, "Mom. Come on, Mom. Get up. We're going to lose."

"We'll pick this up later." Kurt grinned. His wink stole what was left of my breath. He leaped up with the grace of an athlete and offered me his hand. Hand in hand, we scrambled up to Abby and then, with her between us, raced to the top and hopped onto the old school toboggan held ready for us.

"Lean left," Kurt called. I leaned left, Abby leaned right.

"Other way," I yelled just as Kurt hollered to lean right. I panicked and leaned left. Next thing I knew, I was airborne. I landed with a soft splat in a snowdrift. I scrambled to my feet and started running after the sled. There was no way I'd ever catch up, but the timer didn't stop until all team members passed the finish line. Ten feet from the end, I leaped in the air and took an enormous dive and slid on my belly across the finish line to the crowd's raucous cheers.

Abby and Kurt raced toward me and helped me up. "That was insane," Kurt chided with a grin, slinging his arm around my waist.

"You're crazy, Mama." Abby stared at me with wide eyed awe.

"Well, it was faster than running." I winked and laughed. I was going to be stiff and sore tomorrow, but it was worth it for a better score. And to have Kurt's arm around me. I fit perfectly at his side, like we were meant to be together.

In the end we were far from first, that went to the burly dudes, but we were well above last. I was looking forward to the tree decorating contest on Tuesday. At least I wouldn't get the stuffing knocked out of me and I'd get to bask in my daughter's happy smiles, and be close to Kurt for a little while longer. Because, though I hated to admit it, I was falling for this handsome billionaire and almost beyond caring that he had money to burn.

Chapter Eleven

Kurt

Sunday evening, filled with exhilaration after our semi-successful toboggan ride, I loaded a tree on top of my SUV and drove into town. We'd tried a number of times to mesh our schedules, and today was the day. I'd finally get a closer look into Darcy's world.

Mrs. Sharp had given me her spatial requirements and asked me to choose for her. I spent way longer than I should have choosing a six-foot Scot's pine. It was uncharacteristically important that Darcy and her family be impressed with the tree. We never sold a bad tree, ever, but somehow, in my mind, Darcy's family needed the best.

I lugged it up the outside back steps to the apartment above the coffee shop and knocked.

The door flew open and Abby hollered, "Yay. Mr. Kurt is here. He brought a tree."

Darcy urged me in from across the room. I leaned the tree in the corner and shed my coat and boots. The apartment was small. One open, rectangular room held the living area, dining area, and a tiny galley kitchen. Three doors led off to the left. I assumed two bedrooms and one a bathroom. Who shared a room?

Despite its miniscule size, the entire place was probably smaller than the living room in my condo, the apartment was cozy and welcoming. Tiny though it was, it was neat and well laid out. Garlic, cheese, and tomato sauce danced across my tastebuds making me salivate. Whatever they were cooking smelled delicious. Under it all, I detected chocolate and cinnamon.

"Come see my room, Mr. Kurt," Abby demanded.

I glanced at Darcy who looked amazing in her snowflake print sweater and black leggings that clung to the length of her thighs. She shrugged and I followed Abby across the small space.

"Guess which room is mine." She wiggled up and down like I couldn't answer fast enough.

Through the doors I could see a set of bunk beds in one room, and a single bed in the other. I pointed to the bunks. "This one."

She laughed. "No, silly. That one is Mom's and Grandma's. They share. I get my own. Come see." She dragged me inside.

The tiny room had barely enough room for a dresser and bed. Toys and dolls were lined up neatly on the flat surfaces. "Lookit." She pulled out a trundle bed. "I even have a special bed for sleepovers."

"Wow. You are a very lucky girl."

"I love my room," she whispered, "but sometimes, I wish Mama had her own room and didn't have to share with Gramma."

"That's a lovely thing to wish for. You're a very sweet girl," I praised her generosity.

Who could live like this? Three people in a space barely big enough for one. I'd grown up in a modest home. We weren't rich, neither were we poor. We had everything we needed and plenty of space to grow. Here was a little tyke who was enthralled that she had a trundle for her guests. Darcy was raising her right, despite the lack of room. I suppressed a wince at how judgmental my thoughts sounded.

I thought of my condo. Four bedrooms, three baths. A chef's dream kitchen even though I rarely cooked. Spacious and luxurious. Perfectly appointed. Designed within a millimeter of perfection.

And lonely as hell.

"Okay, Munchkin," Darcy said from behind me. "We better eat if we want to decorate the tree tonight."

Trees usually needed to stand for a day or two before decorating to allow the branches to settle. I'd chosen one that was standing, unwrapped, in the lot rather than selecting a bundled up one because Mrs. Sharp had invited me to dinner and to help decorate. I probably could have negotiated it into two meals, but that hadn't sat well with my conscience, despite wishing it were feasible. I liked Darcy, I was coming to crave the peace I felt when she was around, and wanted to spend more time with her, but I didn't want to force the issue.

"Let me put the tree in the stand before we eat," I suggested. "That way the branches can settle a bit."

I carried it to the corner where a decorative metal stand waited. I held it upright while Darcy tightened the support screws. Beyond the fresh scent of pine, I could just make out her sweet floral scent. It reminded me of a meadow of flowers blooming in the sun.

I had a sudden vision of Darcy and I sitting on a quilted blanket in the sun, surrounded by wildflowers, holding hands. I had to remind myself that while I was on sabbatical in Salvation, I had no intention of remaining. Sure, I was ready to seek a new adventure career wise, but I wasn't looking for a wife.

We laughed all through dinner and made plans for future contest events. Since I was detail oriented, I would be responsible for placing candies on the gingerbread house according to Darcy's design.

"Are you artistic?" I asked. For the life of me, I couldn't remember what she'd done in high school. Some of our options had included art and music. I had taken electronics and auto shop.

Beverly laughed. I was finally remembering to call her by her first name as she kept requesting. "Artistic? My girl here can draw like a master. She teaches art classes at the community center every weekend. She even runs summer art camps." Pride rang in her voice.

Abby bolted from the table and came back carrying a sketch book. "Lookit," she thrust it into my hands, narrowly missing her milk glass. I let out a relived breath. We didn't need another food disaster.

I looked up. Darcy was bright pink.

"I don't think so, sweetie. But thank you. Art books are private. How about you put it away?" I suggested.

"It's okay," Darcy said. "There's nothing to be embarrassed about in that one."

Implying that she had some work she didn't want to share. Interesting. The more time I spent with her, the more intrigued I became. I studied her face. She glanced away and looked back. She gave me a decisive nod.

I opened the front cover and nearly lost my breath.

"That's Santa," Abby exclaimed. "From the mall."

Indeed, it was. Darcy had captured his likeness in a way so real he seemed to come alive on the page. I could almost feel the roughness of his beard and hear his laughter.

"This is incredible." I flipped through the pages. Abby with Santa. The crowd at the mall. A group of people barreling down the hill at the sled race. A Christmas tree. I flipped again and gasped. Ethan and Owen were perched on Santa's lap with conspiratorial grins on their faces. Santa looks slightly aghast.

I held up the book so Darcy could see. "Can I buy this one? My sister will love it."

"What? No. I don't sell my work."

"Please." I'm not above begging. "She'll love it. It would be a better gift than whatever my assistant chooses for her."

"Tell me you don't make your assistant do your Christmas shopping." She frowned and her mother laughed.

"I do. Please, sell it to me."

"No." She looked thoughtful for a moment. "But, if you do your own shopping this year, I'll give it to you."

"But she's already started." Lame excuse but I don't care. I'm not a good shopper. I never was. Some people have the gift for choosing presents. My gift was making money.

"That's the deal." She resumed eating and I let the subject drop.

Later while we were stringing lights on the tree she said, "Have you reconsidered?"

Inspiration struck like lightning. "You help me shop, and I'll do my own shopping." I threw it out like a challenge. I saw how she tackled the race today; she had a competitive streak and I wasn't above playing on it. I'd get to spend more time with her, and I'd get my drawing.

"How many gifts?"

Darcy Sharp was no dummy.

"Mother, father, four grandparents, two sisters, one brother, two nephews, and one niece."

"And your assistant does all that? She's a saint."

"She's very well compensated, but I probably owe her a raise now that I think about it. Is it a deal? We shop together. I get the picture."

"Okay. Deal." She thrust out her hand and we shook to seal our agreement. "Make a list with names and ages, favorite colors, and interests. That will give us an idea what might work for each person. And let me know what your limit is."

I was about to say there was no limit but realized that money was tight for her. Otherwise, she wouldn't be sharing a room with her mother. It wasn't like Beverly was in need of attention or care. She was a happy, healthy woman running her own business. Living with her mother must be a necessity for Darcy. She probably didn't make much as a cashier. "I can do that," I squeezed out at last.

Darcy turned on a holiday play list and sang and danced her way up and down the stepladder as she decorated. Her mother helped Abby with the lower branches while Darcy belted out *Rockin Around the Christmas Tree* like a pro. She was beautifully uninhibited; unlike anyone I've ever known. I worried she'd tip the ladder so I held it steady as she shimmied up and down. Unlike my office trees, or the tree my maid set up at the condo, this one was delightfully mismatched and disorganized. Macaroni angels hung alongside antique glass balls. Ribbon, popcorn, and beads served as garland. It had regular balls, Daleks, starships, cookies, dried roses, and tinfoil stars. Captain Kirk hung between the Hulk and Baby Groot.

The crowning glory was Hermione in full Hogwarts regalia holding her wand aloft. Darcy set the topper in place and stepped off the ladder. I pulled it aside so we could see the tree clearly. "Ready?" she asked.

I had no idea what I was supposed to be ready for, but I nodded anyway.

She walked to the corner and set her hand on a light switch. "One, two, three." She hit the switch and the tree came to life. It glowed with brightly colored lights and Hermione's wand shot glittering fiberoptic stars over it all. I had to admit it was magical. Peace and happiness crept over me along with a sense of satisfaction and relaxation. Darcy was good for my wellbeing.

"Perfect," I said, no longer looking at the tree. I can't stop staring at the absolute joy on Darcy's face. What was it about this woman that was so irresistible and compelling?

Chapter Twelve

Darcy

Tuesday, the contestants were split into groups to decorate trees in the senior center, the lodge. the school, and the lobbies of all five local churches. Each group was given a tree, a box of random decorations, and a group of helpers to work with. We were sent to the senior's center where we were lucky to be paired with our, now retired, former high school English teacher who had always adored Kurt. Kurt had her and her cohorts laughing and giggling the entire time. He really had a generous heart.

Because he was tall and we didn't have a ladder this time, Kurt did the upper section of the tree, Abby the bottom, and I handled the middle. We all worked within the guidance of our seniors. It was fun. A group of grade two students, led by Santa, came through to just the entries. Somehow, we took first in the tree contest.

Santa pulled me aside and asked if I'd seen any signs of miracles yet. Laughing, I told him no. The guy really got into the whole Santa gig. If I closed my eyes and squinted just right, I could almost believe he was the real deal. Santa and Abby had a whispered conversation that set her to giggling happily. Later, I saw Santa talking to a frowning Kurt. I would have loved to hear their conversation. I rarely saw Kurt frown.

We collected our Christmas cookie reward and headed for home. Abby snoozed in the back seat. The fact that all these holiday activities tired her out was a blessing. She went to bed on time and didn't get up a dozen times with questions. December was a tough month for parents with children who believed in Santa and exhaustion sometimes helped. "You looked upset with Santa," I said to Kurt, after confirming Abby was out cold.

Kurt grunted. "He refused to tell me what I should buy the boys for Christmas. He said he was using their ideas himself and had none to spare."

"Aw, poor little Kurt," I teased. "You'll have to come up with ideas on your own."

"No, I won't. You get to help me." He flashed me a grin and turned his attention back to the road. Light snow drifted down and turned everything into a winter wonderland.

Except the roads that were a slushy mess. "I'm off tomorrow morning. Do you have time to shop?" he asked.

"As long as I can do some of my own shopping at the same time, sure. Wednesday is my day off. I'll pick you up at nine. I drop Abby at school at eight-fifty."

"Or, I'll pick you up at nine."

"Why?" I squinted at him, trying to figure out what was going on in his thick man-skull.

"Because I was thinking we could run out to Upper Ridge and see what the mall there had." He said it like the answer was a no brainer.

"Or, we could search the shops here...you know, shop local. Then, when we run out of places here, we go further afield." My tone was a bit belligerent, almost daring him to defy me. Not enough people understood the value of shopping local.

"Fine. You pick me up, but when the time comes to leave town, we're taking my SUV, not your little skateboard."

"There is nothing wrong with my car."

"I didn't say there was, but it's small, my legs are long, and frankly, it didn't have the best safety rating when it was new, let alone fifteen years later."

Lord, save me from men who think they know everything. Even if he might be right.

Simple as that, I found myself in his SUV on the way to Upper Ridge. Early in the day, we exhausted the meager offerings of Salvation. At least in his opinion. We had found gifts for his sisters. The kids and grandparents were proving more difficult.

"I was thinking about a good bottle of Scotch for the men."

"Wow. That's a lot of thinking," I teased. "What did you get them last year?"

He coughed and his cheeks pinkened. "Top shelf rye whiskey."

I smacked his arm. "Then no, we aren't buying booze again. Think about it. Think hard." I leaned back and crossed my arms over my chest.

Upper Ridge is larger than Salvation and has two decent sized malls. I was praying he'd find something here, because the next step would be a mega-mall. Malls made me jittery. It was probably related to the fact that before Abby, I shopped as I pleased. My career back then brought in plenty of money. Now, things were tight and I had to account for every penny that left my wallet.

We climbed out of the car and dashed through the frigid air into the mall. Minus thirty Celsius is entirely too cold for me. "What's the plan of action?" he asked.

"Check our coats and hit the stores one by one until we have what we need."

I barely resisted the urge to roll my eyes. Inside, I shucked of my jacket and tucked my scarf into the sleeve. The air was toasty warm and smelled like coffee and spices. Everything was bedecked in greenery and sparkling baubles. It was a stereotypically mall, but charming all the same.

"We can't shop first," I teased him. "First, we find coffee and brunch, maybe just a cinnamon bun. Then, we shop. But only after you make a list of a few gift ideas. Honestly, Kurt, I thought you'd have done that by now."

"I can get behind the coffee, but not the list."

There was a twinkle in his eye as he looked at me. I had a hunch he was pulling my leg and wasn't as opposed to being prepared as he claimed. I would expect a successful businessman to be used to working a plan.

We settled in to a booth in the food court with our coffee. I had a cinnamon bun; he had a breakfast sandwich. We were barely seated when "Santa" showed up. I'd recognize him anywhere though he wasn't in his suit. The guy really got around.

"Look at you two together," he exclaimed. "Mind if I join you?"

I glanced at Kurt who shrugged. "Why not? Please join us, Santa."

"Thank you, and don't be silly, call me Nick when I'm off duty." He set down his tray. Tea, milk, and cookies. He was really carrying this charade to the extreme.

"So, have you finished your shopping yet?" he asked.

"I'm almost finished, but I don't have many people to buy for," I said.

"Just Abby, your mother, and a couple close friends. Have you gotten the man in your life something special yet?" Santa, Nick, asked.

I choked on my coffee. "No man in my life."

Santa, I just couldn't call him Nick, was sitting beside Kurt and gave me a wink Kurt couldn't see. "Are you certain there isn't *anyone*?" he probed.

"I think I'd know," I mumbled through suddenly dry lips. It wasn't the first time I imagined myself with Kurt. He was strong, kind, handsome, generous. He had a good sense of humor. Honestly, except for his money, he was the perfect man.

"How about you, Kurt? Is there a special lady in your life?" Santa asked, leaning forward, and tilting his head so he could see Kurt's face.

Kurt looked at me for a full fifteen seconds, I counted, and a slow smile spread across his face. "There is someone with potential."

Santa patted him on the back. "Atta boy. Knew I could count on you."

Kurt sputtered.

"You should look at the house on Martingale." Santa said. "The big brick one. It's got six bedrooms, tons of rooms for kids. The backyard is enormous. It has a solarium and an indoor pool. It's a great place to raise a family. It's back on the market again, I hear."

"That's a great house. I went to a tea there once. Incredible layout and the solarium is a plant lover's dream. Abby swears she'll own it one day. Though with her current plan to be a teacher, I don't know how she'd ever afford it."

"I'm not sure I'm staying in Salvation," Kurt said. "But I'll keep it in mind."

"You do that. It's a lovely home in need of a family to bring it joy." Santa stood. "Now, I have to order reindeer feed and get myself to Santa's village. I can't disappoint the children. You two take care and keep your eyes open to possibilities and to the miracles of Christmas." He winked and strolled away. For the first time in my life, I thought a stroll looked smug.

"He's a character," Kurt said.

"That he is." I finished my coffee. "You ready to roll? I'd like to get home early if I can. Mom's a great sitter, but I prefer that she not have to take Abby to work with her more than necessary."

"I'm ready. Let me clear the tray and we'll be off."

We hit a bookstore first and he found his father a 1st edition of a herbology book. In the new book section, he found one on growing specialty roses for his mother.

"I've got an idea," he said excitedly. "Why don't I make this a reading Christmas. I can get everyone books!"

"Are they all readers?"

"All except the boys, and they should start."

"Do you know their genres or favorite authors?"

His elated expression dropped. "No," he sighed.

"Keep thinking. You can do this." We checked out the entire mall, waved at Santa as we passed his village and hit the toy store last. Kurt spent a fortune on games and new gaming systems for his niece and nephews. One system for each.

"You're frowning," he said as we carried the packages to the SUV.

"Don't you think you went a bit overboard?" It was none of my business but I was curious, and a bit upset at how easily he threw money around.

Chapter Thirteen

Kurt

It felt like Darcy was judging me. No, she was judging me. And for something that was really none of her business.

"No, I don't think I went overboard. I have money to spare. I want them to be happy. Christmas is a time for magic and if my money makes them happy, it makes me happy."

"How much time do you spend with them," she asked, staring at me over the hood of the SUV. Her expression was accusatory and maybe a bit disappointed.

I suppressed a wince. I rarely saw any of my family. This month, and next, when I was home to rest, was the exception. I'd like to spend more time with them, but I had a company to run. A company that had been running fine for a full month without me. I hired good people and they knew when to call, and when to solve the problem themselves. I had trained them all to call in an emergency, preferably if they had a potential solution in mind. Giving them free rein to find solutions made them more invested in the company. It had paid off well for me and for them.

"I don't spend as much time with them as I should," I admitted.

"Wouldn't that be a better gift than toys they'll discard in days or weeks?" She climbed into the SUV. I followed and started the engine. It blew warm air on us. We hadn't been inside long enough for the engine to cool off fully.

She had a point. My siblings were always inviting me to visit. I paid for us all to take a family vacation every year. Shouldn't that be enough?

"Look at it from a child's viewpoint," Darcy said gently. She gripped my forearm. "Time passes so slowly for kids. Months that pass by in a blink for us feel like an eternity to them. I remember being a kid and waiting for Grampa and Gramma to visit every summer. I only saw them once a year. They lived too far away to visit more often. It felt like forever between visits and every year they changed so much. It broke my heart every time they left."

She pulled out a pot of lip balm and began applying it with the tip of her finger. I followed each stroke with my eyes, her statement instantly forgotten. Her lips were luscious and tempting. I wanted to devour them.

Truth hit me like a brick. I didn't want my siblings' children remembering me for what I gave them. I wanted them to remember my time with them. And I wanted to impress Darcy Sharp. I wanted to be the kind of man she could fall for. Certainly, I was falling for her upbeat attitude and caring heart.

Her generosity reminded me of my mother. As did her ability to make me reconsider things with just a few words. Beyond that she wasn't like anyone I'd ever met. She almost glowed with kindness and positivity.

"Maybe you're right," I admitted after way too much time had passed. "They need me more than things. Should I take some of the gifts back?"

"Entirely up to you. You could save them for birthdays if you didn't want the hassle of the returns line during the holidays."

"Maybe I'll think about it. Why don't we check out the other mall and see what they have for my last few gifts? What do you need to get?"

"There's a custom knitter with a shop on the outskirts of town. I'd like to stop and see what she has, if it isn't too much trouble. I'd like to get something there for Mom and Abby. She does the cutest penguin hats that Abby will love. I meant to order online and forgot."

"We can do that. What's Santa bringing Abby?" I probe. I'm curious to know everything about Darcy.

"A season pass to Heritage Village. She adores the vintage rides and games. It's a great place to spend time together. Their Christmas displays are incredible." Her voice sparked with enthusiasm that warmed me right through. "It's a gift she'll love and a gift for me too, because it gives us bonding time. It's a bit greedy from my end. If she wouldn't love it to death, I'd feel guilty for getting myself a present."

I wasn't a greedy man, but her confession of guilt hit me hard. I spread my money around freely, but never with that much thought. Somehow, I thought bigger was better. That's why we took all the trips. Darcy make me realize that the family loved the trips, not because we went away, but because we were all together. This straightforward, easy-going woman was teaching me so much.

Funny because even as she made me uncomfortable about how I did things, she filled me with a sense of peace that I couldn't deny and was quickly coming to crave. For the first time I could remember the tight band around my chest had eased. Darcy Sharp was good for my health. Last night, when I'd taken my blood pressure, it had been at a record low, almost within a normal range. Then, I'd fallen asleep thinking of Darcy and had the best sleep I'd had in months. I hadn't woken until my alarm went off at eight. I *never* sleep past five.

The second mall was busier than the first. I wanted to cut and run and get my assistant to order the last few gifts. Only Darcy's opinion of me kept me going. Two hours later, I was finished. Shopping completed, and finished as in exhausted.

"Just a second," Darcy said as we walked past a furniture store. "I'd like to check out lamps if you don't mind."

We went in and she made a beeline straight for the lighting department. I lagged behind, looking around. I knew where to find her and I wasn't going to be long. Part of my mind was rolling around Santa Nick's idea of moving to Salvation. I could run my company from here and be closer to my family. Or, I could sell it off. I'd pondered moving on to something new more than once. I love the creative part of my business, and office routine was growing old.

I needed something else. Weirdly, though I hated it as a teen, I was thoroughly enjoying working in the garden center and could see myself taking over when my parents retired.

I paused beside a dining room suite. The solid wood table expanded to seat sixteen and had matching oak chairs. It was perfect for the expanded eating area Mom had added to her kitchen. She was always grumbling about not enough space for everyone. Eating on a makeshift table and folding chairs, like we had when Darcy's family came to dinner, was ridiculous. This set would be ideal, and she'd love the matching cabinet for her *good* dishes.

I flagged down a salesperson and began the purchase.

"What are you buying?" Darcy asked when she returned with a lamp box in her hand.

"A dining room suite for Mom. She'll love it."

She glanced at the price tag and winced. "Seems a bit extravagant."

I bit my tongue. Part of me wanted to tell her to mind her own business. The rest of me didn't want to fight with her. "Mom's going to love it. That's all that matters." The words came out with a barking angry tone that made her wince.

I understand that when you had little, purchases like this seemed outrageous. But when you had it all, the expense was nothing. Different perspectives. Still, I dislike being judged and having my generosity seen as a flaw.

"I'll meet you at the front," she said with a frown, and walked away.

"Do you still want to go ahead with the purchase?" the salesman asked. "Your wife doesn't seem happy with the idea. It's not a good idea to annoy your wife. Trust me, I know." His voice was filled with wry humor.

"She's not my wife. Yes, I'm buying it." My response was probably a bit belligerent. I made the purchase and arranged for delivery on the morning of Christmas Eve. I felt both guilty and pleased that my money got me exactly the delivery I wanted. The guilt part was Darcy's fault.

The ride to the knitter's place was stonily silent. Darcy gave me the address; I punched it into my phone and nobody spoke but the GPS. I wanted to shake Darcy's shoulders and rattle some sense into her. Money meant nothing to me. My family was important and this would make Mom happy. It was exactly what she wanted and it was well above her budget.

I scrubbed my fist against the ache in my chest. So much for Darcy being calming. I wasn't one to get angry, I usually rolled with the flow. Which was why I was startled the first time I had chest pain and rushed myself to emergency.

"I'll wait in the car," I said as we pulled up before the shop. "Take your time. I'm not in any rush." I turned up the radio and leaned my head back and closed my eyes, pretending to relax.

"I'll be quick." She hopped out of the car and hurried inside.

I sat fuming about her attitude toward how I spent money. What did it matter to her? I'm ashamed to say I managed to work myself into a bit of a fit by the time she came back ten minutes later.

Once again, we drove in silence. I didn't ask about her purchase, and she didn't offer anything. The air between us was thick with tension and something close to anger. I stole glances at her as I drove, though it was hard. Winter driving took full concentration. Each glance cut into me. She was hurt and upset. She was still frowning when I dropped her off at home. The pain in my chest intensified as she walked away.

Chapter Fourteen

Darcy

"Thanks for taking me shopping," I said as I climbed out of his SUV before he unbuckled. I grabbed my packages. "I'll see you at the next event." I couldn't get away from him fast enough.

All the way home I fumed. I thought Kurt and I were building something between us. Something that felt an awful lot like love. The past three weeks had been incredible. Laughing together. Playing together. Spending time at competitions and together as friends. Abby adored Kurt. I was just thankful that it was three days until we competed again. With only two tasks left, we were within reach of the prize. The prize was small, just a weekend at a hotel in Upper Ridge with all meals and some passes to local attractions included. It would be a fabulous way to bond with Abby.

The mini-trip was for all members of a team. That meant two rooms, so we'd be alongside Kurt for the weekend we selected. Now, the idea of being close to him for that long made my stomach hurt. I didn't want to have this mountain of unsaid words between us.

We had gotten along well, except when it came to money.

Wasn't that what all couples fought about? Religion, money, and sex?

Religion wasn't an issue. Kurt's family attended our church. Sex? Ha. We weren't even close to that, though my overly fertile imagination had a few ideas it would like to test drive, and unless I missed my guess, Kurt felt the heat too. That left money.

What a doozey!

Today had cemented the fact that Kurt and I were too far apart to ever build something together. I blinked back tears. I didn't want to be this attracted to him, or to be having thoughts of building a future, but the danged man had stolen into my heart somehow.

I climbed up the steps to the apartment and let myself in. I hid the gifts in my closet and flopped down on the bed. Tears leaked out of my eyes and ran down my face. Stupid man. Stupid money.

I really should have gone downstairs and brought Abby up. It was well past dinner and close to her bedtime. Instead, I took ten minutes to wallow in self-pity. I felt like something fragile had broken inside me. Like the stem snapped off a rose. Or a shattered crystal vase. Could it be my heart?

I knew the companionable time I'd spent with Kurt was over. If that wasn't enough, I had to deal with him for the final events. He was too honorable to quit and disappoint Abby even though we'd had a falling out. Chalk up another reason to fall for him.

Chapter Fifteen

Kurt

We met at the edge of Emmerson's Park the next night at six-thirty. Glowing Christmas lights hung from the lampposts and trees. A cheery fire burned in the center of the park. Once again, food trucks dotted the perimeter and offered tasty treats. The night was warm for December, only minus six. It was the perfect night for outdoor games.

The scheduled event was an outdoor obstacle race. There were thirty stations. Each member of the team had to complete an equal number of tests. It was up to us to decide who did which station. The course was cordoned off, but we were able to navigate around the outside and discuss each challenge. We'd be timed for each section and an aggregate time given. Extra seconds would be added for challenges not complete in a set amount of time.

We took our assigned timetable and headed to the first challenge. I studied the competition. "I don't think there are as many people here tonight," I commented.

"Definitely not. It seems like the competition thins with every event."

"I think we can win this. We've divided things up well." I gave her my best smile, hoping to thaw the ice around her heart. It was Christmas, the time of forgiveness, and hadn't Santa Nick said to watch for miracles?

"I don't know if we can win, but I'll do my best," Darcy answered a full minute later.

"I'm eager to try my stations. I'm going to kill this, and I know you'll do great too. Both of you." Darcy squatted down to talk to Abby. Clearly my failed attempt at a conversation was over. I had totally screwed it up with Darcy. She was barely speaking to me, and then only grudgingly.

I inhaled a calming breath. It stalled in my throat with a stab of pain. It hurt to breathe. Careful not to be seen by anyone in my family who had come to watch, I massaged my chest. This was not another mini-infarction. It couldn't be. I'd cleaned up my diet and I was working out.

"Are you okay?" Darcy asked. "You look pale."

"Just tired," I lied. "It was a long day. I was up late last night doing paperwork."

She gave me a sideways look that said she knew I was lying.

"O-kay. If you're sure."

"I'm sure." I wasn't sure, not by a long shot. But I didn't know what to say to placate her anger. No, not placate. Not mollify. More...bring us around to friendship and understanding again. I needed her in my life.

"Okay, Abby, you can do this," Darcy pumped her up before she began the long crawl through a narrow tunnel. She was the only one of us who would fit.

Abby raced through the tunnel with speed and agility that startled me. I waited at the end to high-five her. She threw herself at me and clambered up my body like a monkey. "I did so good," she crowed.

"Yes, Munchkin, you did. I'm proud of you. I ruffled her hair." She leaned over and rested her head on my shoulder like she belonged there. My heart cracked open a little. I needed to find a way to make a relationship with this family work. My heart had been stolen and I wanted it back.

***

Abby

The games were so much fun. I don't think we are winning, but Mama says we're doing well. The bestest part is spending time with Mr. Kurt. I just know that Santa sent him to us. He's gonna be my new dad. I always wanted a dad.

Mama's being grumpy. I think she's mad at Mr. Kurt. I need to make her not be mad any more. She's looking at him with her angry face. She used to look at him with that squishy, icky, I like you face. How can he be my daddy if she doesn't talk to him?

I need to talk to Santa again. He can fix this. He can do anything.

"Mr. Kurt?" I ask. "Do you like Mama?"

"Of course, I do, Munchkin. I'm on your team, aren't I?" His eyebrows got grumpy.

"No! Not like that." Why didn't he understand? "Do you like-like her. Do you want to marry her and become my dad?"

His eyebrows lifted to the top of his head.

"It isn't that easy. When adults are friends, sometimes it turns to like-like, to love. But there are always problems to be sorted out."

My eyes got wet and my stupid nose started to run. Mr. Kurt didn't love us. Christmas was ruined.

***

Kurt

Shoot. Abby was going to cry. What did I do? I couldn't tell Darcy what she said, could I?

"Hey. Your mom and I are friends. Friends fight sometimes. We'll figure it out."

She sniffed loudly. "Then you'll be my dad?" she asked with too much hope in her voice. She was killing me. Literally. Something stabbed into my chest with knife-strike precision. My knees buckled.

I set her on the ground and grabbed her hands. "Honey, we'll work this out. But not right now. Go get your mom. Bring her here." Darcy was talking to the judge about something before we moved on to the next challenge.

"Are you okay?" She blinked up at me like she didn't understand what I wanted.

"No. Get your mom." A dropped to my backside in the snow and struggled to get my breath. The squeezing in my chest doubled and my arm went numb. I managed to turn her toward Darcy before I lost all strength.

I was going to die!

It's true what they say. When you're dying, your life flashes before your eyes.

Mine was a continual loop of me. In my office. Alone.

I had nothing.

No friends. I didn't have a family of my own. I had money.

Nothing else.

God, I was a billionaire and I was a total failure.

Darcy had it right. I threw my money around like it meant something. I used it instead of being there myself. So help me God, if I lived through this, I was a changed man. I'd use my money for good, and be there, in person, for the people I loved. That included Abby and Darcy.

I squeezed my eyes shut against the pain. Physical and mental.

"Kurt," Darcy's voice penetrated the agony. "Are you okay?"

"H-h-heart," I squeezed out through my gritted teeth.

"You're having a heart attack?" she asked. "Call 911," she screamed, much too close to my ear. "Hold on tight, Kurt. Don't leave us. We need you."

"For the contest," I quipped. "Can't. Win. Without. Me." I gasped between each word.

She laughed hysterically. "No. Idiot. In our lives."

"What's going on?" I recognized Santa Nick's voice.

"He's sick," Abby wailed.

"Heart attack," Darcy confirmed.

"Try and relax," he said. He pressed his hand into my chest and the pain ebbed immediately. It wasn't gone, but I could breathe a bit better.

"What?" I asked. "How?"

"Christmas magic." Santa winked.

Sirens sounded and came closer by the second.

"Darcy, you were right."

"Shh," she said soothingly. "We'll talk after you see the doctor. Okay?"

"Now." It was still hard to talk but I needed to get this off my chest. No pun intended.

"You're right-"

"Kurt," she snapped. "Shut up." Tears ran down her face. "Just get better, okay."

"Anything for you. I'll even take back the gifts."

"Idiot." Her laugh was watery. Paramedics pushed everyone aside. I realized my entire family stood in a circle around us, keeping everyone else at bay, protecting me. I didn't deserve their caring. Not one bit.

"She's with me," I told the medic.

"No, sir. She has to find her own way to the hospital. We don't have time to coddle your wife."

"Not my wife, yet." I turned to my mom. "Bring Darcy to the hospital. Watch Abby for her." Every word out of my mouth was agony and came with a groan of pain.

"I'll drive," Santa Nick declared.

They loaded me up and we drove off. This was it; I was going to die and I hadn't even told Darcy that I loved her. She was right. I was an entitled idiot. If I die, I swear on Santa and the North Pole that I'm coming back to haunt Darcy, just to spend eternity with the woman I love.

Chapter Sixteen

Darcy

A million regrets raced through my mind as the ambulance pulled away. I'd been too harsh with Kurt over money. I'd let my own insecurities cause me to judge him wrongly. Maybe he wasn't perfect, but he was perfect for me. For us.

Like it or not, I'd fallen for Kurt years ago, before he ridiculed me at his prom. I never stopped caring for him, even when my heart was broken. Even while I was engaged to another man. Now, he was going to die not knowing how much I loved him. I accused him of wasting his potential time with his family and I'd done worse. I'd pushed the man I loved right out of my life.

Thank heaven he was with us when he had his attack. At least now he had a chance of getting proper care in time. How did a thirty-six-year-old man have a heart attack? Was this his first?

It wasn't. More than once I'd seen him massaging his chest. Heart attack? Heartburn? Sweet heaven, I hope it's just a false alarm.

"Come on, Darcy," Santa said. "I'll take you to the hospital. We're meeting Kurt's family there." Half in a daze, I followed him to his car.

"Mama, is Mr. Kurt gonna be okay?" she asked, her voice trembling.

"I sure hope so, baby-girl." She didn't object to the name she'd recently told me she was too old for. That was a testament to her concern for Kurt. A concern that echoed mine. "He'll be at the hospital soon and they can fix him right up."

"Then can he finish the contest?" She blinked up at me. We'd climbed into the backseat so I could comfort her while Santa drove.

"Maybe. It depends on how sick he is."

"Will he get better and be my daddy?"

I blinked stupidly. "What?"

"I asked Santa to send me a daddy and Mr. Kurt came to play the games with us. I love him. I want him to be my daddy." Tears swept down her cheeks and dripped off her chin. I glared at Santa in the rearview mirror. He shrugged eloquently, as if this wasn't his fault.

"Sometimes things happen that aren't supposed to be together. Mr. Kurt is our friend. That should be enough."

"But I love him," she wailed.

I pulled her into my arms. "I do too," I admitted softly.

Santa, Kurt's entire family, Mom, Abby, and I sat in the emergency waiting room. Waiting to hear how he was doing.

My friend Morgan, who was finally back at work as a nurse, having defeated the bug ailing her, popped her head out to say, "Kurt is doing okay. He's out of immediate danger and is getting some tests." She'd never have gotten away with the announcement in a city hospital, but this was Salvation and sometimes rules slipped...in a good way.

I couldn't sit still, so when Abby finally dozed off, I set her on a chair, her head in Mom's lap and started pacing. Up and down the short hallway, round and round the tiny waiting room. I felt like I'd wear a hole in the industrial lino floor.

I'd been such a fool. What did it matter if Kurt wasted his money? It was his, not mine. He was still a good person. He was helping his family run the greenhouse during the busy holiday season. He spent time with his family, and with us. I had no right to judge him based on my own life.

Maybe I couldn't waste money right now. But would I do any different if I was rich? I'd probably give large, extravagant gifts to. I certainly never worried about before

Abby. What a fool I'd been. I pushed away the man I loved, and yes, I did love him. What if I'd ruined my chances with him, my chance for happiness? All because I was jealous of his financial position.

With every minute that ticked by, the ache in my heart grew. I'd blown away something special.

"Darcy," Morgan said nearly an hour later. "Come with me. Kurt would like to see you."

"Maybe his family should go first," I said, glancing at his distraught mother.

"He requested you." She turned to his family. "He's going to be fine. I promise."

Audrey's shoulders slumped in relief and a watery smile flashed onto her face. "Go ahead, Darcy. I'll wait."

I rushed over and hugged her. I realized how hard it must be for a mother to let someone step into her place. Especially with her oldest child. "Thank you."

"About time you got here," Kurt grumbled when I entered the room.

I rushed to his side. "Are you okay?"

His face turned pink and he looked away.

"What?" I probed. Why was he embarrassed all of a sudden? An idea hit me. "It wasn't a heart attack, was it?"

The nurse checking his IV laughed.

"It looks like it was just a panic attack," he admitted. "But they're keeping me here overnight just to be sure. They'll run more cardiac tests tomorrow. I have a history of heart issues."

I stared at him. "You might have mentioned that." I swatted his arm.

"It was one very minor incident. I took a sabbatical to rest. Doctor's orders. Now, after this scare, I'm retiring. I'm going to help at the greenhouse full time. I don't want to experience that ever again."

"That's a big step," I warned. Hope bloomed in my heart and a rush of love washed over me. "Can you give up the CEO life that easily?"

"Yes!" He grinned. "Being back in Salvation has taught me a few things. I need a slower pace. I'm over the whole CEO life. I don't want it anymore. I'm selling my company. Most of all being here, and this *incident,* taught me that I need human contact. I need a family of my own."

"Oh," I whisper, almost breathless with hope and anticipation.

"It taught me that I need love. I need you, Darcy. You and Abby. In my life and in my heart." He clutched my hands in his. "Darcy, will you marry me?"

Sparks flashed before my eyes and I swear on the North Pole that I heard bells ringing with joy. "Yes. Oh yes. But only if you get out of here and change your lifestyle. I won't leave Salvation."

"You don't have to." He laughed. "I'm buying the house on Martingale that Santa Nick mentioned. That's going to be my, our, new home. If you'll have me."

"I will. I already know it's okay with Abby. She adores you."

"I know," he said wryly. "When she asked me to be her daddy, I had a panic attack. For a while, I thought it was a heart attack and that I was going to die."

He looked so chagrinned that I had to laugh along with him.

"Man, we're going to have to straighten you out," I teased.

Epilogue

Abby

Santa held my hand and we peeked through the doorway at Mom and Mr. Kurt. He was going to be my new dad! I giggled. I was so excited. It wasn't even Christmas yet and I got almost everything on my list. I got a dad; we were getting the big fancy house I love. Mr. Kurt's family would be my family. Maybe I'd even get my puppy. There were still *days* to Christmas.

"Thank you, Santa," I said and hugged his legs.

"You were a very good girl this year. Now, go see your mom."

"And my new dad," I whispered, almost scared if I said it too loudly it wouldn't happen. I stepped into the hospital room. When I looked back to say bye, Santa was gone.

I guess it's close to Christmas and he has lots of work to do. After all, he had tons of kids to get gifts for so they could all be as happy as me.

Books by Katie

<u>Coyote Creek</u>:
A Lesson in Love 1
A Secret to Shatter 3
A Heart Torn Apart 2
A Melody for Christmas 4
A Surrender so Sweet 5
A Place Called Home 6
A Love to Rebuild 7
Coming Home for Christmas 8
Coyote Creek Box Set 1
Coyote Creek Box Set 2

<u>A Silver Fox Christmas:</u>
Their Christmas Heart
Their Christmas Love
Their Perfect Christmas
A Silver Fox Christmas Box Set

Hearts Haven:
Building Trust
Running Home
Saving Grace
Heart's Haven Box Set

Coming Soon:
Cappuccino Mugs and Fire Fighter Hugs
Carly's Heart

Three Moon Falls:
Water Magic
Fire Magic

Stand Alone Books:
Cupid's Charm
Hearts in the Spotlight
To a Tea
Bulletproof Heart
Fake Dating at Half Moon Bay
Gingerbread Dreams
Christmas in Silver Creek
Sleigh Bells Inn
Protecting Josie
Rekindled Fire
Matchmaker Christmas

Books with Heat:
Corralling the Cowboy
Cornering the Cowgirl
Tessa's Trio
The Gift

About Katie O'Connor

Best-selling author Katie O'Connor lives in Calgary, Alberta, Canada. She married her high school sweetheart and is living her happily ever after. She is the mother of two grown daughters and is extremely proud of her five grandchildren.

She is the founder of The Write Chicks, a private romance writers' group set up with the sole purpose of supporting each other's writing career. Currently, she is chapter president of the Calgary branch of the Romance Writers of America. In the past, she's been their secretary and has also served on the organizing committee for When Words Collide, a reader and writer conference in Calgary, Alberta.

Katie's career path has been long and twisted, with most of her life devoted to her family. She's been a waitress, chambermaid, cashier, store manager, as well as a lab and X-ray technician. She's been a small business owner and is an avid quilter and crafter.

She's dabbled in writing since high school because something drives her to create stories. She swears it's impossible for her NOT to write. Unsatisfied with one genre, Katie writes contemporary romance, fantasy/paranormal romance, and romantic suspense.

She believes in all things magical, including dragons, fairies, UFOs, ghosts, and house pixies. But most of all she believes in love, romance, and hope.

www.ingramcontent.com/pod-product-compliance
Lightning Source LLC
Chambersburg PA
CBHW020139180626
46810CB00004B/1643